The Oldest One

Dorothy Holder Jones

THE
OLDEST
ONE

Funk & Wagnalls Company, Inc., New York

In memory of my sister
VIRGINIA FRANCES

Contents

The Oldest One

1

The Interview

"Fran," Mrs. Rogers called across the rows of tables and drawing boards, "would you stop by my desk a moment before you leave?"

Brushing her long, blond hair aside, Fran Avery looked up from the sink at the rear of the art lab where she was rinsing her water-color brushes.

"Yes, ma'am," she replied, wondering why she was always the last one to leave when she tried so hard to be punctual. She glanced anxiously at the clock over the doorway. Oh, dear. It was three-twenty, and she was supposed to be at the Prince Studio at four. Since yesterday, when she had arranged the interview with Mrs. Prince, Fran had felt as if her heart was racing ahead of the clock, propelling her there, beat by beat.

Stacking her paint box with her books, Fran hurried to the front of the room. Mrs. Rogers, who was one of her favorite teachers, was dark-haired and pretty. She wore a distant, dreamlike expression, Fran had observed, until she began discussing art. Then, she became quite animated.

"Fran, my dear," the woman began, "I was going through the entries for the art-scholarship contest, and I can't find yours. Aren't you planning to enter it?"

Fran swallowed hard. How could she explain her situation to this teacher who thought art was the most important part of one's life?

"I didn't fill out an entry blank, Mrs. Rogers, because I— well, I can't really afford to go to art school even if I should win." There, she thought, I've said it—once and for all.

Mrs. Rogers was frowning now. "But I explained to all my students that you could earn your expenses. The scholarship covers full tuition—"

"I—I know," Fran conceded. "But, Mrs. Rogers—" she steadied her voice, "after I graduate, I'll have to go to work, anyway."

The teacher stared at her thoughtfully. "I remember now. Your father isn't living, and there are several children in the family."

"Yes, ma'am." Fran straightened her shoulders until she stood every fraction of her five-foot, five-inch height. "I'm the oldest. I have two sisters and a little brother. My mother sells dresses at Draper's. We get Social Security, too, but there's not much left for extras."

"But it's such a shame, Fran. You're so talented! I feel it's my duty to encourage students like you, who have a definite spark."

"But, Mrs. Rogers," Fran declared, "you haven't met my sisters. Diane's twelve. She's a natural dancer. And Linda, who's ten—well, she can make music out of anything. They're really talented, and that isn't just my idea. Remember last year when the Woman's Club put on 'The King and I'? Well, Diane made the finals in the tryouts. She sang and did a ballet dance she'd made up herself. Everyone said she was terrific, and they were amazed that she'd had no training. And our church pianist thinks Linda—"

Fran stopped abruptly, realizing that she must sound like a stage-struck mother instead of an older sister. Besides, she told herself, Mrs. Rogers would never consider ballet lessons and piano lessons and a complete overhaul on the family station wagon as important as an artistic career. So Fran decided to keep her personal plans to herself.

The teacher was smiling pleasantly. "You must be a devoted sister, Fran. But I won't take this as a final answer. The deadline date is—let's see, October thirty-first, over a month away. And it will be almost a year before the winners are announced. You can't lose anything by entering it, my dear, except a little time working up something to send in."

"I'll think about it," Fran promised, sneaking another look at the clock. "Is that all you wanted, Mrs. Rogers?"

"Yes, dear."

Fran hurried down the hall, past chattering students and slamming lockers and open doorways that echoed the sounds of Friday-afternoon freedom at Waverly High. Any other day, she might have been thrilled over Mrs. Rogers' interest in her, but now the interview and its promise for the future crowded out everything else.

She had almost forgotten to tell Millie McArdle that she wouldn't be walking home with her today, until they collided just outside the English classroom.

"Oh, Millie," she had gasped, flustered. "Don't wait for me today. I've got an errand up at the shopping center."

Millie's gray eyes had brightened. "Oh, shopping? Date?"

"No, nothing like that." Faced with her friend's puzzled look, Fran added, "I might as well tell you because if I get the job, I'll really be broadcasting the news!"

"A job? Oh, Fran, not during your senior year! This summer it was all right working on Saturdays to pass the time, but now— Why, you won't have enough time as it is!"

Fran stiffened, remembering the frustration she had felt last summer. Millie had been her dearest friend since first grade, but she would never understand Fran's problems. Millie was an only child and she had everything, even an extension telephone in her room.

Skipping down the last flight of stairs, Fran discovered Joe Collier waiting just outside the door. Her racing heart skidded to a sudden stop. The late-afternoon sun brought a coppery glow to his hair and softened the tan he'd acquired during his lifeguarding hours at Waverly Park the past summer.

She had known Joe for years, and once they had even built a tree house together. Now that he was almost eighteen and a senior and considerably handsomer and infuriatingly indifferent, she had difficulty keeping her voice steady and her smile casual.

"Joe!" she exclaimed. "I thought you had football practice this afternoon."

"On Friday?" His brown eyes searched her face. "With a game tonight?" His impish grin hadn't changed at all, she thought, as he added, "I suppose you expect me to drag you to the sock hop afterward!"

"Thanks for your usual tactful offer," she retorted playfully, "but I'll relieve you of the strain. I—I won't be going to many dances this year. In fact, I won't even keep up with the team. I'll probably be working."

"Working?" He stared at her in astonishment. "But you worked all summer, Fran—well, on Saturdays, anyway. I'll bet you banked enough to live high the rest of the year."

"I spent that money," she reminded him, "for school clothes for my sisters and myself. But there are other things more important—"

He chuckled. "To girls? What else is more important than clothes? Except boys, of course."

"Well," she replied defensively, "I'm determined that Diane should take ballet and Linda piano lessons. And our car needs repairing, you know. And if I expect to go to evening college next year, I'll need tuition."

"Boy, listen to Miss Martyr herself! Fran, you're not the only girl with two little sisters and a brother." His tone was sober, now. "You don't owe them everything."

Fran squared her shoulders. "I'm not being a martyr! I'm trying to use plain, common sense. My mother's too busy feeding us to worry about the future, so it's—well, it's up to me. By the time Diane graduates, she might decide to teach dancing or go on the stage or something. And Linda could put herself through college playing in dance bands!"

"Or get married," Joe put in dryly, "and then you'll regret all your sacrificing."

"Go ahead and scoff at my fancy dreams, but it has been done before. And if they do marry early, well, at least they'll have some kind of training to fall back on if they ever need it. Anything would be better than—" She caught herself, remembering that she had never said these things even to her mother.

Joe shrugged. "OK. It's a great noble gesture. But I think you'll quit. It's just too hard to keep up your grades and all the social life without adding a part-time job during your senior year. I know I'd sure hate to be working now. I'm carrying trig and physics, plus English and Spanish, and football for dear ol' Waverly. I'm glad Dad can afford a generous allowance."

After they parted, Fran crossed the street. She forced herself to push away Joe's discouraging opinion. Maybe she was being dramatic about the urgency to earn some money. Maybe the children didn't really need the things she hoped to buy for them. Maybe they would soon tire of ballet and piano lessons.

Yet, every payday when she and her mother huddled over the kitchen table, trying to stretch the dollars to cover the bills spread before them, Fran came to the same conclusion: one salesclerk's salary couldn't provide more than the bare necessities for a family of five. Fran had already discovered from occasional baby-sitting jobs and her Saturday job this summer that even a *little* added cash could lighten their load.

Ironically, the taller the children grew, the longer the list of expenses. Even though Diane handed her clothes down to Linda, eight-year-old Jamie needed a new jacket every winter, plus a constant supply of jeans and mittens. All three wore through shoe leather as if it were tissue paper. And food—that really was a bottomless subject.

The nearer her steps brought her to the photography studio, the faster her thoughts whirled. Should she act eager or nonchalant? Should she be reserved or enthusiastic? Oh, dear, would they pay her enough to make it all worthwhile?

Mrs. Prince had urged her to wear her school clothes, but now Fran felt certain that her white blouse and cheap plaid skirt were shabby looking. But, she reassured herself, a few paydays would fill a few gaps in her wardrobe.

Fran had been inside the studio only once. She'd accompanied a friend, Debby Pierson, to pick up an older sister's wedding photos. But she had passed the shop every Saturday last summer on her way to work.

Remembering the quiet, plush reception room, Fran had been enchanted with the idea of working there from the moment she had seen the ad on the bulletin board in Principal Brockmeyer's office last Monday.

"Wanted," the ad had stated, "senior girl with pleasing personality, neat appearance, to work as receptionist in photo studio on afternoons and Saturdays. Must be dependable, willing to learn. Salary commensurate with ability."

It was the kind of position that Fran had dreamed about during those long hours when her feet had ached from standing at the candy counter at the five-and-ten-cent store. Imagine, working at a job where she could sit as well as stand and wouldn't be tempted to stuff herself with chocolate-covered peanuts! Best of all, she'd be gaining experience in a field that, she hoped, might lead to a full-time job when she was graduated next June.

She stopped now in front of the plate-glass window and studied the dramatic arrangement of photos against the dark-green background. Some of the portraits were of Waverly High students; others were of children in the community. Above the entrance swung the impressive black and gold sign "Photos by Prince."

A trio of girls passed her and entered a drugstore just ahead. Fran wondered fleetingly if she would come to regret giving up her afternoons and Saturdays. Of course, helping with the housework and the children at home was rather confining, but at least she could squeeze in personal phone calls and entertain friends who dropped in and watch TV.

Anyhow, she reflected, what could be more confining

than an empty purse? Stepping into the reception room, Fran was surprised to discover that it was no longer decorated in green. Now there were shades of brown blending into beige. Just inside the door was a wide counter of highly polished wood. Mahogany, Fran decided, as she approached it. Against the wall on both sides of the long, narrow room were foam-cushioned sofas in a rich, chocolate brown.

Fran swallowed suddenly as a woman, whom she recognized as Mrs. Prince, suddenly came through a doorway on the right. She wore a green dress, and her black hair was wound into a low chignon.

Smiling radiantly, the woman said, "Good afternoon! What can I do for you?"

"Mrs. Prince, I—I'm Fran Avery." She was startled to hear the words come out clearly. "I was supposed to see you at four."

"Of course. Have a seat, dear, while I tell Mr. Prince that you're here. He'll want to meet you."

She opened the door on the right and disappeared. Fran sank down on the nearest sofa and closed her eyes, trying to steady her pounding heart. I'm here, she thought, on time, and I've introduced myself, and I'm still in one piece!

Mrs. Prince returned a moment later, beckoning Fran to join her at the counter. "I'll need some information. Your address, and at least three references. Then I'd like to show you some of the duties involved. I want you to know exactly what you'll be getting into. A few applicants have already informed me that it looks terribly boring!"

Fran was already having some misgivings of her own. One glimpse at the clutter of manila envelopes and stacks of photos under that polished counter top had made her shiver. Will I have to keep all that in order? She answered the questions Mrs. Prince asked while the woman jotted

notes down on a white pad of paper that was chained to
the base of the telephone.

Fran quickly decided not to give Mrs. Rogers as a refer-
ence. The teacher would probably mention the scholarship
to Mrs. Prince, who would feel guilty about hiring a "talented artist" as a mere receptionist. Instead, Fran gave the
names of her English and home ec teachers and Mrs.
Brantly, her Sunday School teacher.

Two young girls, burdened with books, walked in just
then and up to the counter. One quietly handed over an
envelope. "I like the first proof best of all, Mrs. Prince. I
want three 8 × 10's and twelve wallet size, please."

Mrs. Prince wrote up the order, graciously assuring the
girl that she had made the best choice. "These should be
ready next week. We'll call you."

Eagerly absorbing the procedure, Fran noticed that the
woman wrote the girl's name and telephone number on a
slip of white paper, stapled it to the upper corner of the
first proof, and then placed it on the bottom of a small,
wire basket under a stack of similar proofs.

Mrs. Prince made the work sound simple. "Always remember that the customer comes first. No matter how rude
anyone becomes, never lose your pleasant manner. Answer
the telephone graciously, and take down the names and
phone numbers of all customers who order photos or want
to discuss them with Mr. Prince. Secondly, never commit
Mr. Prince to any photo assignment or appointment until
you consult him. And never quote any prices except those
listed on this chart."

She pushed the telephone aside to reveal a large, white
card, sealed in plastic and taped to the counter top.

"Later," she said, "as you learn the routine, you will be
able to book appointments by phone without consulting
us—that is, for portraits here in the studio."

As Mrs. Prince continued, pointing out other duties, Fran's eyes wandered skeptically over the counter, noting several different wire baskets and the long row of slots stuffed with more envelopes. Oh, dear! How will I ever remember it all?

Abruptly, a tall man, with a ruddy complexion and thick, white hair, stepped up beside her.

"Mr. Prince," Fran blurted, startled.

He thrust a large hand out to Fran, while his wife made the introductions. "So, you think you'd like to be a receptionist!" His voice boomed through the room. His eyes darted from her freshly shampooed hair down to her polished flats. "Well, you'd certainly brighten up the place!" he added.

A moment later, though, he was briskly serious. "There's one question that's most important to us, Fran. Why do you want the job?"

Fran took a deep breath. "Because I—I need it, Mr. Prince." Her voice came out shakily. "I need spending money, and I'd also like some experience. And the work really does look interesting."

He kept studying her face. "It's fascinating work, all right, but hectic at times. You see, Fran, Mrs. Prince has been helping full time since I opened up here seven years ago. But it's too hard for her to help and keep house, too. Her mother came to live with us recently and needs more attention. We've tried all sorts of receptionists—older women, younger women—but we can't afford the salary that seems necessary to employ someone suitable on a full-time basis. That's why we're considering a high school girl.

"Mrs. Prince," he went on, "can handle the work in the mornings, and Greg, our son, comes in from Junior College at about one and stays on for the afternoon. He's out delivering some wedding pictures just now. We need someone from three-thirty until six-thirty on weekdays and on Saturdays from eight-thirty to six-thirty. Those hours are long, I know, but the pay would more than compensate."

Fran quickly dismissed the struggle to remember if she'd ever met a young man named Greg Prince. Instead, she was mentally juggling her schoolwork and home chores, trying to fit them into such a schedule.

"Would those hours," Mr. Prince asked now, "hamper your social life? That's equally important to us. We don't want a girl who'll tie up our phone making personal calls or dash out to meet a date on the dot of six-thirty, leaving a customer standing at the counter."

"I—I don't blame you!" Fran found herself smiling as she replied. "You wouldn't have to worry about my social life, Mr. Prince. I'm the oldest one at home, and I've broken so many dates to stay home and baby-sit that I usually lose a beau before I've even got him!"

To her surprise, the couple laughed together.

"Fran," Mrs. Prince broke in, "does your mother work, too?"

In a quiet, casual way, Fran explained her family situation. Before she could elaborate on her plans for Diane and Linda, Mrs. Prince gently observed, "You really do need the job, don't you, dear?"

Fran felt color flaming her cheeks. "I'm sorry," she blurted. "I—I wasn't trying to play on your sympathy. It's just that—"

"That's all right, Fran." Mrs. Prince patted her arm. "We'd have learned about your family, anyway. It was nice to hear about them from you," she added graciously.

Although the Princes enveloped Fran in their friendly interest, she still sensed their businesslike approach. Mr. Prince began discussing the salary, astounding Fran by what he would pay a high school student. He hastened to point out, quite solemnly, that he expected "quality performance."

Suddenly, he was asking, "Fran, do you still think that you'd like to work for us?"

Fran forgot all her efforts to be poised. Her eagerness came rushing out in a joyous "Yes, sir! I'd really love to!"

2

Explanations!

Interviews aren't so bad, Fran reflected, as she walked away from the studio. All you have to do is relax and behave naturally. Relax? Why, I haven't unwound yet!

At the end of the block, she crossed under the traffic light, still reliving the exciting visit with the Princes. As she turned down Dozier Drive, she realized that it was time to start thinking about her mother's reaction. This was the first vital decision she had ever made without discussing it beforehand with her mother.

"That's exactly why I didn't tell you, Mother," she would say. "I'm old enough to make important decisions

—old enough to take over some of the financial responsibility."

She glanced to her left, to the low brick house where Millie lived. During their grammar school days, she and Millie and Joe had lived on the same block on Sandy Lane. The summer before the three became freshmen at Waverly High, a subdivision of spacious new homes opened up around the corner on Dozier Drive. Soon the Colliers and McArdles moved, bringing their families two blocks closer to the shopping center and the high school, and several steps further up the social ladder.

Fran wasn't ashamed that she was still on Sandy Lane, the only remaining unpaved street in the community. They still had a spacious yard with big trees that gave their home a charm of its own. She didn't mind that her home was a cramped, six-room, frame house, badly needing paint or that there had never been any change in her social status. She had her share of friends and still felt close to Millie and Joe, but she had often thought that they accepted her too easily. They couldn't see how really different her situation was from theirs.

Millie, she thought, was probably secluded in her room, playing records, devouring a mystery novel, and munching on potato chips. And Joe—she glanced across the street at the attractive brick home with sparkling white shutters and breezeway and double-car garage. Joe's jalopy was there, as well as his family's car.

Fran sighed dejectedly. Joe would be off to the game soon, probably taking Millie and another couple along. The thought had nagged her constantly this summer— Millie and Joe. She had begun to suspect it when she realized that Joe never teased Millie, never gave her one of his sugar-coated, uncomplimentary remarks.

Of course, Millie practically lived at the swimming pool

all summer. She kept insisting that she had gone to be around Pete Cassidy and that Joe had eyes only for Fran.

"I know you think he just hangs around you from habit," Millie told her once, "and maybe that's what *he* thinks. But *I* don't think so!"

Well, Fran consoled herself now, I'll be too busy to stand around waiting for Joe Collier to make up his mind.

Little Jamie was in the living room, dressed in full cowboy regalia, lying prone before the TV set. Linda was huddled in a corner of the ragged sofa, engrossed in a fairy-tale book.

Pretty Diane, her golden pony tail bouncing as she rushed up to Fran, blurted, "Where've you been, Sis? It's nearly five-thirty! When you told me to stay home and watch the kids, I didn't know you wanted me to make a *career* of it!"

Fran walked on through the living room toward the kitchen, her sister following. "Fran," Diane persisted, "where were you—talking to some boy?"

Fran tried to suppress a smile. Diane, in her last year of grammar school, had suddenly discovered *boys*. "I'll tell you later, honey. I've got to talk it over with Mother first."

"Oh, glory, a mystery!" Diane exclaimed as she picked up the lid of a pot on the stove. While the steam poured forth, she said, "I peeled the potatoes, Fran, but they keep burning on the bottom. You whip them, eh? Jamie doesn't like my lumps."

"All right, Diane," Fran agreed. "This is fine—and thanks." She glanced at the kitchen table, which Diane had set in her own peculiar fashion. Napkins were placed diagonally and glasses were mid-center of the back of each plate.

From the back of the refrigerator, Fran took the veal patties she had allowed to thaw during the day and put them on to fry. She washed a fresh head of lettuce and, after it had drained, chopped it up in five wooden salad bowls.

When she realized that there was nothing for dessert, Fran thought again about her job. One thing she had promised herself—she would walk up to the bakery every Saturday on her lunch hour and buy something delicious for the weekend.

Jamie wandered in, then, sniffing as he neared the stove. "Goody, hamburgers!" he squealed, lifting bright blue eyes up to Fran.

Fran turned the meat over gently. "No, honey. Veal patties today. And how's my sweet boy been today?" She reached down and patted his soft cheek as he leaned against her skirt. She decided to wait until later to give him a hug. Jamie, whose affectionate ways had made him the joy of the Avery family, was increasingly boisterous and aggressive. At times he rebelled at their attempts to chain him to babyhood when he was going on nine.

"Fran!" Now it was young Linda who came into the kitchen, demanding attention. "Make Diane stop saying I'm fat! Just because I'm filled out and healthy doesn't mean I'm fat! At least," she added impishly, "I'm not prancing around trying to make boys notice me. Fran, did you know that Diane smiles at Kippy every day in the lunchroom? And she's just twelve!"

"I'm going on thirteen," Diane corrected. "Some of the girls in my class wear pink lipstick, but I don't!"

"You don't need any," Fran assured her. "You're pretty enough as you are. Besides, girls like us, with blond coloring, just don't need much make-up."

Fran gave the two a quick appraisal. "And while we're so concerned about appearances, Diane, your bangs need trimming again. And, Linda, we'd better give you a shampoo."

"Tonight?" Diane asked. "Aren't you going to the game?"

"No," Fran replied quietly. "I probably won't go to a game this entire school year. I'll be too busy."

"Doing what?" the girls chorused.

"Cooking!" Fran retorted as she handed each of them a platter to set on the table. "What else?"

"Glory," Diane fumed, "you're treating us like children again!"

A moment later, Mrs. Avery came home. "Hello, dears." She smiled as she entered the kitchen. Wisps of hair had loosened from her blond braid, and her black dress was crumpled. She sat down on one of the kitchen chairs and slipped out of her shoes. "They wanted me to work tonight, but I just couldn't take it another minute. Besides—" She looked at Fran now. "When some girls came in talking about the game, I was afraid you might have a date."

"Fran's not going to date anymore," Linda solemnly announced. "She's doing something that's a *secret*."

"My goodness!" Mrs. Avery turned to Fran in bewilderment.

Jamie hovered over his mother, adding, "Fran's got a surprise!"

Fran shook her head. "I can't discuss it in front of them, Mother. Besides, supper's ready."

During the meal, Diane recounted her ordeal of staying with the children after school, which had so hampered her freedom. Then she recited other problems with girls—and boys—at school.

Linda repeated to her mother her personal disgust over Diane's infatuation with Kippy Hargrove.

Jamie injected a brighter note, revealing his triumph over a new third-grade reader. "And Miss Taylor," he added proudly, "let me read in front of the whole room!"

After the meal, the children took their plates and silverware over to the sink before they left the kitchen. Fran and her mother cleared the other dishes together.

"I'll wash, dear," Mrs. Avery said. "I have to redo my nails tonight, anyway."

Once the others were gone, Fran told her mother in a quiet, calm voice about the ad on the bulletin board at school.

"So, I called up about it yesterday, and Mrs. Prince said she would see me at four. That's where I was this afternoon." But then Fran began to hurry on, explaining it all excitedly. She had eagerly awaited her mother's reaction, but Fran was dismayed now at the strange, horrified expression on her face. "You," Mrs. Avery said in a hoarse voice, "went to see about a *job*?"

"Yes, Mother! Isn't it wonderful? All that money! Why it's twice an hour what I made last summer, and it will be such interesting work."

"But, Fran, your studies— You'd be working about twenty-four hours a week! Oh, honey, it's your senior year. I was counting on your having a lot of good times."

"But, Mother, how can I when I haven't any pretty clothes or extra money? And look what happens when you have to work nights. I had to break half a dozen dates last year when you had to work late and the kids had colds and we didn't want to leave them with a baby-sitter. Since I don't have much time for social life anyway, I might as well do something worthwhile with what's left of my time.

"Mother," Fran went on, pleading now, "Diane is old enough to watch the kids more. And Mrs. Holley is handy next door in case of an emergency. I know Diane and Linda scrap a lot when we aren't around, but it's time they learned how to live together peacefully!"

"I know, dear," Mrs. Avery said thoughtfully, as she slowly swished suds around the meat platter. "Diane is old enough to take over more of your chores. But the money isn't your problem, Fran. You're only seventeen, honey, not much more than a baby yourself."

"A baby?" Fran grimaced. "Mother, I'm almost a woman. You were married at nineteen, so why can't I get a part-time job when I'm seventeen?"

Fran walked over to the dish cabinet and deposited a load of plates, as if to give her mother time to think over her remark. When she returned, she waited, her eyes fixed on her mother's face.

"Fran, it isn't the fact that you'll be working that bothers me. I thoroughly enjoyed the little jobs I had when I was your age. But that was different. I—I didn't work during my last year of school except now and then on Saturdays. Honey, if it's clothes you want, I can get more night work. Draper's will be open three nights a week from now until Christmas. That would give us a little extra money."

Fran turned away, groping for words that would convey her personal convictions without hurting her mother. She could never say aloud that she felt a sense of desperation sometimes, watching her mother come in every evening from a job she didn't like, a job that exhausted her, simply because she had found no better way to support her children. All Fran could do was point out the obvious things.

"Mother," she said now, "I was really thinking of the girls. You know how we've talked about giving Diane ballet and Linda piano. Well, it's time they got started. And we could have the car repaired, so you wouldn't have to ride in that car pool."

The silence dragged miserably. When her mother finally spoke, Fran was startled by her answer.

"Well, when do you start to work?"

"Oh, dear! I haven't really gotten the job yet—for sure. They're supposed to call me sometime before Monday and let me know."

Fran's mother broke into laughter that was mingled with tears. "All this—this shock over a job you don't even have?"

Fran stiffened. "They liked me, Mother, really they did. I could tell."

"Of course they liked you, Fran. How could they help it? But if they haven't told you—"

"It isn't definite, Mother," Fran admitted sheepishly now, "but I had to discuss it with you and the kids and explain the adjustments we'd all have to make."

By then there was no need to call the others. All three were there, anxious and curious, demanding to know Fran's surprise. Fran had scarcely related the plans when Diane and Linda began spending the money.

"Boy," Linda exclaimed, "now I can buy some new clothes and my lunch every day at school!"

Jamie spoke up, insisting that he would now count on receiving an allowance just as his sisters did.

"Glory!" Diane fumed when she learned that all three would be expected to add more chores to their list if they wanted any increase in their spending money.

In the midst of this discussion, the telephone shrilled in the hall. "That's gonna be my job!" Jamie shrieked before his sisters could respond. "I get a nickel for every time I answer, so there!"

The girls giggled, but waited in the kitchen to hear who was being honored with the first call of the evening. Jamie galloped back to them, his face beaming. "Fran, it's a lady— that Mrs. Prince. She wants to talk to *you*!"

3

Fran's First Day

Sitting there at the reception counter on Saturday morning, Fran was still rather giddy from the shock.

"Why don't you come in tomorrow, dear?" Mrs. Prince had suggested the evening before. "You can sort of try your wings? That way you can tell if you'd like the job permanently." Permanently, Fran had thought. Of course I'd like that! But now, if she had any wings, she was certain they would be much too limp to get her off the ground.

Only one customer had come in so far—a young bride. She was back there now in the portrait room with Mr. Prince. After getting Fran settled at the counter, Mrs. Prince had gone out to shop for awhile.

Oh, dear, I've got to stop shivering. There's really nothing frightening about it. She told herself that it was no worse than making a speech during assembly at school.

She smoothed the pleat in her skirt, tugged at a wrinkle in her hose. Then she glanced once more at the wire baskets. She had gone through those already and rearranged all the manila envelopes. Now all she could do was sit and stare.

At that instant, the telephone rang and Fran literally jumped off the wooden stool. She grabbed for the receiver with both hands.

Clearing her throat, she greeted the person on the other end of the line as she had been instructed. "Prince Photos," she said pleasantly, "Miss Avery speaking."

"Oh—Miss Avery," a woman's voice came back. "Mrs. Prince called me the other day and told me my photos were ready. I'm going down to Draper's after awhile, so I'll pick them up on my way. Could you find out how much I owe?"

A quick glimpse at the long row of slots jammed with manila envelopes containing pictures to be delivered at the counter made Fran shudder. "I'll have to have your name, please—and the date, if you remember it."

"Oh, I can't remember the date! But it was about a month ago. The pictures should be listed under Mrs. Tom Whitman, or Shirley Whitman, my daughter. They're her pictures."

Shirley Whitman. The name summoned forth a memory of blond loveliness, the girl voted the most beautiful in the junior class last year. If she couldn't find the pictures by name, Fran told herself, at least she could recognize the subject.

"Hold the phone a minute, please, Mrs. Whitman, and I'll try to get that information for you."

Taking a deep breath, she started sliding envelopes out of

the slots, one by one, just far enough to read the names written on the front. Finally, there was one labeled, "Mrs. Tom Whitman." Below the name were the words "$20.00 due."

Relieved, Fran picked up the receiver and told the woman the amount.

"Twenty?" she replied. "I thought surely they would be more. Well, that's plenty to pay for black and white photos, anyway, isn't it?"

Fran hesitated a moment over a suitable reply. Then she said gently, "I'll leave the envelope out so you won't have to wait." The woman thanked her, and Fran thanked her for calling.

After she had hung up, she sank down on the stool, surprised that her first telephone encounter had been so simple. Now why was I so afraid of that?

The door opened then, and three young girls, attractive in fresh hair-do's and bright sweaters, walked in. The tallest one, who seemed slightly familiar, asked curtly, "When did *you* start working here?"

"This morning," Fran replied in her most pleasant tone. "What can I do for you?"

"I came for my pictures. Mrs. Prince said they were ready."

"And your name, please?" Fran asked graciously.

"Iris Morgan!" the girl retorted. Turning to her friends, she added, "I knew she wouldn't remember me. Sat across from me in study hall a whole semester. Humph!"

"I'm sorry," Fran burst out, flustered. "I recognized you, but I—I forget names sometimes."

"Well, don't forget mine—Iris Morgan!"

Fran stiffened as she turned away to search through the envelopes. No, she thought, I'll never forget your name again. You're one of the rudest persons I've ever met. She forced herself to keep smiling as she handed Iris her change.

When the trio finally went out, Fran let the tears well up in her eyes. Why should I let someone like that upset me? she thought. I'm going to be the best receptionist the Princes have ever had, she vowed. I won't let anyone make me unpleasant!

A young mother with three little girls came in for an eleven o'clock appointment. Shortly afterward, Mrs. Whitman came in for her photos.

Opening the envelope, the woman gasped. "There are only two 8 × 10's here, Miss Avery! Where's the other one?"

Fran stared, confused. "I don't know, Mrs. Whitman," she admitted frankly. She looked deep into the envelope and then read the notations on the white slip of paper attached on the outside. "It doesn't say anything about three copies, Mrs. Whitman. Just two. There must be some mistake—"

Distressed now, the woman explained that she had called Mrs. Prince a few days after the original order was given and asked for one more. Together, Fran and the customer concluded that the second order had been placed in a separate envelope, but a quick search failed to locate it.

"I'll talk to Mrs. Prince about it as soon as she comes in," Fran promised, trying to be soothing. "Then, I'll call you."

As Mrs. Whitman left the studio, Fran tried to regain her composure. She was beginning to understand what Mr. Prince had meant yesterday when he described the work as hectic. Surely, all the customers wouldn't present such exasperating problems.

A moment later, the telephone rang. Fran answered in her most efficient tone.

"Miss Avery speaking!" a familiar voice mocked. "Aren't we grand?"

"*Millie!* How did you know to call me here?"

"Elementary, dear girl. I called to see if you'd like to waste a morning shopping with me, and Diane told me the exciting news. So, maybe we can lunch together. You *do* get a lunch hour in that slave galley, don't you?"

"A half-hour," Fran replied, thinking how glorious it would be. "But I can't go until Mrs. Prince gets back—about twelve-thirty, I guess." Glancing at the clock on the counter, she added, "That's still over an hour."

Fran lost all sense of time, however, after the next person walked in. She was sitting there, shuffling through the envelopes for that missing photo, when a tall young man stopped in front of the counter.

"So, you're Fran!" he exclaimed. "I heard Mom call you last night."

Greg Prince, Fran thought, her heart leaping with delight. He had the dark coloring of his mother, the broad build of his father, and his smile was like a sudden shaft of sunshine pouring into the brown reception room.

"Well," he asked now, "how do you like being a punching bag?"

"A punching bag?" she repeated, curious.

"Sure." He chuckled softly. "While you're being initiated in this trial by fire, you'll get your share of blows—a lot of them to the ego. But once you become a member of this great, universal club known as Public Service, you'll find that there are compensations."

"I'm glad to hear that," she confessed. "I was beginning to regret all my wonderful plans."

As Greg Prince came around the counter, he withdrew a camera from the leather satchel he carried and then an assortment of black and chrome gadgets. "I had to shoot some sorority pictures this morning," he told her. "Nuisance stuff, but it's business."

Fran watched him tinker with the equipment. "Do you take many pictures for your father?"

"Most of the outside work, Fran. Here in the studio, I get the darkroom work." His eyes swept over the counter. "How's business? Seems awfully slow for Saturday."

"Slow?" Fran grimaced, thinking back over the morning. Remembering the Whitman photo, she quickly explained the situation. "Where do you suppose it could be?" she asked finally.

"Hmmm." Greg studied the white slip that Fran had removed from the manila envelope. "Mom must have forgotten to combine the orders. Simple mistake. Let's look up the negative file, Fran, and get to the bottom of the whole thing."

That morning, Mrs. Prince had quickly pointed out the negative file, but there hadn't been time to discuss it. Now, though, Greg Prince explained that the negative of every photo made at the studio was inserted in a small envelope and labeled on the front with the name of the person or family or social group pictured, along with the date it was made and the number of types of prints made from it. These, he said, were filed alphabetically.

After that, Greg opened another drawer full of manila folders that were also indexed alphabetically. "This is the personal-record file," he told her. "It's sort of a cross-file for our negatives and photos—as well as our bookkeeping. If we didn't keep it, we'd be in one colossal mess!"

He took out one of the folders and showed her the list of pictures made for a family named Baker. There were dates and prices listed on a large white card for baby photos, graduation and wedding pictures, and family groups.

"Why, it's really a family record!" Fran exclaimed, as the details suddenly came into focus.

He grinned. "Sure. If Mrs. Baker should call in and

want another copy of a certain favorite picture, we would be able to find it, regardless of the date. Commercial studios file negatives by numbers that they print on the bottom of each negative. But that way, our customers would have to keep a record of those numbers if they ever wanted to reorder copies of certain photos. Part of our stock in trade is the family appeal—serving a community. We make it easy on the customer and complicated for ourselves."

Fran was so engrossed in Greg's explanation that she forgot about the counter and the customers. When Mr. Prince suddenly spoke nearby, Fran turned in surprise.

"Don't let me disturb you two," he said, "but I've been waiting to see Greg. Son, is the Statham wedding scheduled for tonight?"

The young man frowned. "It's next Saturday. Why, Dad?"

The mother with the three small girls walked out from the hallway. Mr. Prince cordially bid the customer good-by. After she was gone, he gave his full attention to Greg.

"Well, Mrs. Statham called the house early this morning," Mr. Prince went on, "after you had gone. She said the flowers wouldn't be ready on time so we'd have to take all the pictures after the ceremony."

"But that was already agreed," Greg spoke up. "Her daughter didn't want any pictures made before the wedding."

Mr. Prince rubbed a hand over his face. "Frankly, I'd forgotten that. When she called, all excited about it, this morning, I assumed the wedding was tonight."

Oh, dear, Fran thought. It was complicated!

Greg stepped over to the counter and scanned the appointment book. "No, Dad, it's scheduled for next Saturday night at eight. It must be just a mix-up with the florist—two weddings in one evening, no doubt."

After Mr. Prince disappeared down the hallway, Greg turned to Fran. "This happens now and then, especially during the top wedding months—June, July, and September. In a community like Waverly, with only a couple of churches and one local florist, two weddings on one Saturday night in the same church give the florist and the poor photographer some timing problems. There's hardly time to decorate the altar for the second wedding because of the pictures being taken at the end of the first wedding."

"Oh," Fran said quietly, "I see."

"Now, back to the Whitman picture," he said, reopening the negative file. But a careful investigation of it and the personal files and the appointment book for several weeks back failed to reveal the whereabouts of the missing portrait.

Mrs. Prince came in shortly after twelve, and Fran immediately told her about the Whitman photo.

"Goodness!" the woman gasped. "I remember now—but I don't believe I ever wrote it down! Well," she shook her head in dismay, "we'll have to rush another 8 × 10 through for her—a special order. My mistake should be a good lesson for you, Fran. You can see why it's terribly important to write everything down. Trust nothing, *nothing*, to your memory."

An hour later, Millie appeared, gray eyes twinkling. "Wow!" she whispered across the counter so the customers, who were now collecting around the reception room, couldn't hear. "You certainly picked a plush place to slave. Sorry I'm late. Can you leave now?"

"Yes, but I'll have to tell Mrs. Prince."

Fran hurried over to the hallway on the extreme right of the reception room that led to the dressing room and then to the portrait room. Beyond them was the darkroom where Greg was now printing pictures. Hanging on the door was a sign reading, *Don't Open! Genius at Work!*

Mrs. Prince was in the portrait room, discussing a pose with a mother and her teen-age daughter, while Mr. Prince waited patiently behind the camera.

"Mrs. Prince," Fran asked hesitantly, "may I go to lunch now?"

"Of course, dear! I'll be right out."

Walking down to the sandwich shop, Millie plied Fran with questions. "Think you'll like it, Fran?" she asked finally. "Better still, will they like you?"

"How can I tell, Millie? They're such lovely people. If they didn't like me, they'd probably just tell me quietly that they had decided to get someone older."

Millie looked distressed. "Fran, I didn't mean to upset you. They wouldn't fire you on the first day, anyway."

"I'm not upset, Millie," Fran assured her gaily. "I'm trying to be sensible. It's just a trial day. They could call in a different applicant every day if they wanted to. I still don't see how they had enough time to call all my references last night—"

"Elementary, Fran. All they needed was one glowing report, especially from a school teacher. Teachers' standards are so high."

Years ago, someone had inserted a sandwich shop between the shoe-repair shop and the corner drugstore. Millie and Fran, as well as others in the school crowd, favored it because of the generous supply of pickles and potato chips served with every order.

The juke box was blasting away as the two entered, and booths were brimming over with teen-agers. Millie found an empty booth, slid into it, and slipped off her jacket. Fran pushed up the sleeves of her sweater and began studying the menu.

After ordering cokes and ham and cheese on rye, Millie began on all the news. "You missed a terrific game last night, Fran. I'm almost glad you did. Joe made two touch-downs, but I'm sure you've heard about that. But did—did anyone tell you that Betsy Parker ran right out on the field after the game and kissed Joe right in front of every-body? Fran, I'm scared. That girl has been batting her lashes at Joe for weeks now, but I was hoping that I was just imagining it."

"Betsy Parker?" Fran asked weakly, as she felt a lump in her throat. Betsy had violet-blue eyes and black, wavy hair and her father was a local dentist. She had lovely clothes, her own convertible, and an allowance large enough to pay Fran's salary at the studio every week. And here, she thought, I've been worried about Millie and Joe!

"You heard me," Millie replied dejectedly. "Fran, you'd better start treating Joe—well, special, or she'll have her hooks into him but good!"

Fran stiffened. "I can't, Millie. I won't have time to worry about Betsy or bat my lashes at Joe. If I get that job, I'll be working about twenty-four hours a week."

Millie was aghast. "Fran, that's a whole day out of every week! Worse, it's twenty-four waking hours! Oh, you're just being a martyr to your family. You're so wrapped up in those kids that you can't even enjoy life any-more."

Fran stared at her friend. "But they *are* my life. I enjoy them—every waking hour!" She knew, of course, that Millie would never really understand how she felt about her family. An only child like Millie just couldn't know what she was missing.

Quietly, though, Fran explained. "Millie, don't you see that I'll be doing this as much for myself as for them? I'll have some money for clothes and movies. Besides, I want to do things for the kids. Sure, it would be fun to have more money so I wouldn't *have* to work. I'd like to have time to go to parties and have more dates. But the funny thing is, I really don't miss dates. The kids are so entertaining. I suppose I would change my mind if someone—well, suddenly noticed me. Really noticed me."

Millie was toying with a paper straw. "Believe it or not, I think I know what you mean. It's always such fun at your house. But there's something peculiar. My argument is sound, and your argument is sound. Somewhere, there must be a compromise."

"I've been thinking about that. And it's elementary," Fran added playfully. "I'll just date on Sunday afternoons."

4

Defending her Decision

Fran was up to her elbows in dishwater when Linda led Joe
Collier into the kitchen. "Here's Joe," she announced super-
fluously. "I didn't know you had a date with him, Fran!"

"I didn't," Fran replied, her face stinging. Why were
ten-year-olds so blunt? When she glanced at Joe, dressed
in his Sunday suit, his red-gold hair sleekly smooth, she
gasped, "We didn't have a date—or anything, did we?"

"Not exactly." He leaned against the sink cabinet, his
face troubled. "Didn't Betsy Parker get hold of you this
afternoon? She was trying to call you."

"No. Why?"

"Well, she's throwing a party—one of those last-minute things. She told me if I saw you, to bring you along."

"I see," Fran said quietly, understanding all too well. Turning to Linda, she inquired, "Did Jamie answer the phone this afternoon?"

Linda replied by yelling for Jamie, who came rushing into the kitchen, his face puckering. Even Mrs. Avery opened her bedroom door and called out to them.

"It's all right, Mother," Fran told her. Then she turned to Jamie. "Honey, did a girl call me several times this afternoon?"

"Yeah," Jamie nodded. "She told me she would call you back. And she did."

Linda grabbed his arm in exasperation. "Boy, you're some help! Fran was getting an invite to a party! When are you going to learn to take down messages, or tell Diane and me about these things?"

Jamie's distress was swiftly becoming defiance as he glared back at Linda, his fists clenched.

"Never mind, Jamie," Fran said, patting the child comfortingly. "You didn't know, and it's not really important."

She persuaded the two children to return to the living room. By now, tears were threatening. She was tired and confused. Worse, though, was the haunting question she wanted to ask Joe: Why didn't *you* call me about the party?

"Well," he asked now, "can you make it?"

She struggled to steady her voice. "I'm afraid not, Joe. I have a thousand things to do. Even if I'd known ahead, I probably couldn't have been ready in time. I didn't leave the studio until after six-thirty."

Diane, who had walked into the kitchen at that moment to begin drying dishes, broke into the conversation. "She had to wait a few minutes to get paid. They gave her a check." Diane tossed her pony tail demurely. "Joe, Fran's got a new boyfriend, and is he cute! His name's Greg Prince!"

"Diane!" Fran exclaimed. "He's one of my bosses and that's all!" To Joe, she explained, "That was her conclusion, not mine. All I did was describe him. Besides, he must be at least twenty-one!"

Joe chuckled. "I know. He was a three-letter man at Waverly a few years back. Nice-looking fellow."

"Yes," Fran agreed, "and he was awfully kind to me."

"Well," Joe finally said, "guess I'd better get along. Sorry you can't make it, Fran. It should be quite a ball."

Fran found her voice long enough to thank him for dropping by. "And thank Betsy for inviting me. Maybe next time."

Joe left as unceremoniously as he had come. Fran finished up the pots and pans, scrubbing them furiously now. Diane prodded her with questions until Fran ordered her to stop.

When the children came back to the kitchen, Diane turned on Jamie. "From now on, little boy, you do something harmless like taking out the trash or putting out milk bottles. Linda and I will answer the phone!"

"Stop nagging him!" Fran protested. "It isn't the first time I've missed getting a call—or going to a party. Besides, I've been home over an hour. She could have called again or at least told Jamie to have me call her." She didn't add that Joe could have called, if he had really cared enough.

Diane's blue eyes widened in a look of horror. "Glory, Fran, do you think Betsy didn't want you to come to the party?"

"Diane, I don't really know what happened. And I don't care!"

Mrs. Avery appeared then, wearing a smock over her house dress. "Did I miss Joe altogether?"

Diane related the episode almost word for word. "But

she's not going, Mother. She's too busy, and she thinks Betsy just invited her to be polite or something."

Fran's mother gave her a bewildered glance. "But why, Fran? I can handle everything tonight."

"Mother, I just don't feel partyish. I didn't do my nails last night, and I've been so busy this week that I haven't had time to take the hem up on my blue silk dress. And I've got the devotional in Sunday School tomorrow."

Mrs. Avery took the dish towel from Diane. "You've helped enough, Diane." She smiled. "I want to talk to Fran now—privately."

After Diane left, Mrs. Avery began solemnly, "You see, Fran? This is why I don't want you to work. You just can't cut out parties at your age. Turning down a date now and then is one thing, but if you can't find time for a party or two with your friends, well—"

"Mother, I wish I could convince you that I really don't mind. I mean, what's a few hours of sitting around having laughs compared to working at the studio?" Fran recounted some of her day, partly to explain what being a receptionist at a photography studio was like, partly to prove to her mother that she actually enjoyed it.

"Of course," Fran admitted, "they might not call me back. But I know they liked me or they wouldn't have spent so much time showing me everything. Mother, if I see that I just can't handle it all, then I'll quit. At least, I'll have a little money to show for my efforts."

"You won't push Millie and Joe out of your life, will you, Fran? You three have grown up together."

Fran emptied the dishpan slowly, watching the suds oozing down the drain. "If I grow away from them, it won't be because of my *job*. I just don't have much in common with them now, Mother. Millie has no responsibilities. She's just a gadabout. And Joe— well, he treats me as if I'm an old shoe." Her voice wavered as she added, "Not that I care."

"I know, dear," Mrs. Avery said pityingly. "It isn't easy. I mean, being fond of a boy who doesn't seem to return your feeling. It happened to me once. I was miserable for a whole year, but then I found someone else who did care. Joe is fond of you, though, Fran," she added quickly. "Otherwise, why would he keep including you in his plans?"

Fran squeezed her eyes shut to keep tears from spilling out. Do I show it that much? she wondered. But then, she supposed that mothers sensed such things more than others did. Forcing herself to sound gay, she said, "I'm not really sure how *I* feel about Joe, either."

Fran spent the evening getting her limited wardrobe in order. When the Late Show came on, she settled in the living room and raised the hem on the blue silk dress that she had worn to parties for the past two years.

Sunday afternoon, which she divided between her family and school work, Fran felt as if her heart were suspended in air. The Princes had to call her. They *must!*

Late Sunday evening the phone rang just as Fran was passing through the hall. Mrs. Prince sounded breathless as she said, "Fran, dear, we just got in. A young niece of mine in Rockmart got married this afternoon and asked us to take her wedding pictures. I wanted to make sure that you understood that we expected you back tomorrow afternoon. That is, if you want the job."

"If I want it?" she burst out. "Oh, Mrs. Prince, I've never wanted anything so much!"

When she reached the living room where her mother and Diane were watching TV, Fran was surprised to see them grinning.

"We heard," Diane exclaimed. "You got the job!"

Fran didn't need to question her mother's approval. Her eyes were proud above a radiant smile.

Monday morning was unusually hectic. After her mother left for work, Fran hurried the children through the morning routine, issuing a long list of instructions as she did so.

"Now, Jamie," she reminded him, "let the girls answer the phone. Linda, stay close to home and mind Diane. And Diane, put more potatoes on to cook this afternoon—and don't be too bossy!"

Hastily, she kissed all three, then rushed out of the house. After she turned from Sandy Lane into Dozier Drive, Joe rolled his jalopy out of his driveway, opening the door as she neared him. "Hop in," he said, grinning. "The fare's ten cents for riders who work steadily!"

As usual, Fran climbed into Joe's car only seconds before Millie burst from her house and sprinted out to join them, her jacket and hair tossing about.

"Oh, Fran," Millie began immediately, "you missed the party of the year Saturday night." She combed at her hair now, using the mirror of her compact to guide her efforts. "Betsy sent us on a scavenger hunt. Imagine!"

Fran gripped her books tighter as she forced a smile. "I'm sure it was fun," she replied, trying to avoid even a trace of resentment.

"And the refreshments," Millie raved on. "Wow!"

"It was a ball," Joe spoke up. "But let's not overdo it, Millie. After all, Fran sat home admiring her paycheck."

Fran replied playfully, "It was an awfully good Late Show. One of those old Clark Gable adventure things."

Millie wrinkled her nose. "Not again! I've missed the last three!"

"You see?" Fran chuckled now. "There are compensations!"

:

Once her classes had begun, Fran dismissed the weekend and postponed thoughts of the afternoon. She intended to enjoy the day and make the most of every minute.

Just before lunch, Laura Maynard, one of Millie's friends, cornered Fran in the hall. "What's this I hear about you getting a job? I was planning to make you chairman of the scenery committee."

"Oh, dear," Fran said. "I completely forgot the Dramatic Club and the scenery I promised to help with this year. I'm sorry, Laura, really I am. Last spring—well, I just didn't know I'd be working this year."

Laura pretended to pout. "You could at least have waited until next June before you went after the filthy lucre! Goodness, I'd like to make some money for myself, but being president of the Dramatic Club is a responsibility, and *I* don't intend to shirk it."

Fran lifted her chin defiantly. "Laura, I have a few responsibilities myself—two sisters and a brother." After she spoke, Fran felt her face stinging. Laura was one of six children, but her father was a successful engineer and the Maynards lived in style. "I'm afraid I won't have time now, Laura. If Mrs. Mason asks about me, you can tell her for me." She turned then, wanting only to escape the uncomfortable encounter.

She had almost regained her composure when Beverly Brown confronted her in English class. "So, you're working at Prince's Studio. Well, la de da! They should pay you well. They charged my cousin a hundred bucks for one portrait last year. It should have been tinted in gold!"

Fran stammered around, trying to justify such a price. She finally managed to say, "It must have been something really special."

By the time she reached art class, Fran's ego felt rather battered. She was baffled, too. How did the school grapevine spread news so fast? Even Mrs. Rogers had heard.

"Fran," the teacher inquired as she beckoned her over, "is it true that you've gone to work at Prince's Studio? How will you have time to do anything worthy of that contest?"

"I don't know," Fran confessed. "I'll have to see how things work out, Mrs. Rogers."

Considering the confusion she felt, the afternoon at the studio went smoothly. Several customers called for proofs; others came in to pose. Greg Prince arrived at about four and settled down in a corner of the reception room with one of his textbooks. Shortly afterward, the phone buzzed. It was a girl with a bubbly voice, asking for Greg.

"That's my girl, Barbara," he said. "But don't worry, Fran. After tomorrow, I'll be getting personal calls in the darkroom. I'm having another phone, a private one, put in there."

It was later that Greg mentioned that he and Barbara Lane were engaged.

The evening at home was chaos.

Diane had scorched the potatoes, and Jamie whined over the "brown spots" that Fran was unable to remove after they were mashed. Linda had quarreled with a friend at school, and she insisted on relating every insult. Diane reported that her charges had misbehaved almost constantly and therefore she expected more pay for her afternoon's work.

Diane further complicated the evening by fuming because her mother refused to buy her a certain white pleated skirt. "But it was on sale," Diane protested, "a whole dollar off! And with your discount—"

"Even with my discount," Mrs. Avery replied calmly, "the skirt is too expensive. And a white tissue wool is much too impractical for school wear."

"Glory," the child choked out, "everyone has one—but me!" She turned pleading eyes toward Fran. "You'll buy me one, won't you, Sis?"

Fran shook her head. "No, Diane, you might as well understand right now. I'm not working to buy you any luxuries, just advantages, and there is a difference. If Mother doesn't think you need one, then I certainly wouldn't get you one. Which would you rather have— several ballet lessons or a white pleated skirt?"

Diane was pensive. "When I'm practicing ballet, I wish I had lessons. But tomorrow, when I go to school and see the other girls, I'll wish I had that skirt!"

Mrs. Avery joined Fran in a quiet chuckle. "Diane," her mother said, "you've just discovered one of the trials of human existence—wanting to have your cake and eat it, too!"

After Diane was sufficiently soothed, Fran went to her room and attacked her homework. At ten o'clock, the house grew still. Fran went into the living room and apologized to her mother for forgetting to help her get the children to bed. "I got so busy, I just worked right on through!"

"Fran, honey, I don't expect you to help with everything. If you don't do anything except your homework and getting your clothes ready for the next day, that's enough!"

Fran sighed tiredly as she curled up in a corner of the sofa. "Mother, there's no reason why three hours at the studio should paralyze my entire evening. Look at all the time I used to spend on the phone and watching TV. I should be able to do all the things I did before and work, too. Maybe," she added thoughtfully, "I need to get organized, the way you are."

Her mother's voice was solemn. "Don't get too organized, dear. You'll get more done with a schedule, but life's more fun when you don't stick to one too rigidly."

"I can believe that," Fran said, closing her eyes.

5

A Busy Saturday

Saturday morning began like many October mornings, brisk and unsettling.

When Fran reached the studio at eight-thirty, she felt as if she was a late arrival to an important meeting. All four of the brown sofas were filled with a collection of mothers and children, from a bouncing baby to two primping teenagers.

"Good morning," Fran greeted them bewilderedly. How could so many people manage to come to the studio so early? She pulled the appointment pad over and tore off Friday's sheet. "Eight-thirty A.M. Saturday—the Bradley cousins."

She glanced back at the group, aware now of the resemblance. She was familiar with family-group pictures, but this was beyond her experience.

Mrs. Prince stepped out from the hallway just then. "My," she declared, "I feel like the Pied Piper this morning. Come on in, you ten beautiful Bradleys!"

While Fran stared in amazement, six youngsters and two women holding two babies, got up and followed Mrs. Prince down the hall.

Once the room was empty, Fran took advantage of the quiet and began to check over the pictures on the counter. There, attached to the top of a stack of photos, she found a note:

> *Fran, I filed the negatives on these proofs, but didn't have time to put them in envelopes. I'll let you have this honor. And please call all these customers and tell them their proofs are ready. Thanks! Greg.*

Fran read the message three times, glowing with satisfaction. Already Greg considered her capable of handling such a task. She went through the fresh proofs carefully, removed the white slip on which the name and address was written, and inserted the maroon proofs into fresh envelopes bearing the letterhead of the Prince Studio. Lastly, she stapled the white address slip on the outside of each envelope, fastening the flap down securely as she did so. With that chore finished, she turned to the phone and dialed the first number listed on the top envelope.

"Mrs. Bailey," Fran said pleasantly when a woman's voice answered, "this is Miss Avery at Prince's Studio. Your proofs are ready."

"Oh, fine! How did they turn out?"

"Turn out?" Startled by the unexpected question, Fran

reopened the envelope and studied the poses. "They're nice," she said. She didn't mention all the wrinkles around the eyes, because the smile was so pretty. "Yes, they're really nice."

The woman said that she would try to come by for them that morning, and Fran hung up the receiver, marveling at how simple the task had been. And, my, how efficient she felt!

The next number she dialed rang several times, but no one answered. The third number brought forth a husky male voice. Once Fran related the details, the young man replied, "Well, Mom's at the store right now, but I'll have her call you. What's that number?"

After Fran recited it, the boy chuckled. "Say, maybe I'll call this number myself sometime. You sound kinda cute!"

Fran put the receiver back with a slam. Her face flamed as she wondered if he had really been serious. She had hardly dismissed that embarrassing moment when Greg walked in. He stopped at the counter to check the order pad and the appointment calendar.

"Good morning, Greg." She smiled, partly in appreciation of his immaculate blue-black suit, white shirt, and blue tie. "You must have an important assignment."

"Hi yourself, Fran!" He gave her one of his dazzling smiles. "It's just a business luncheon, but a few aldermen will be there."

"Really?" It was vague, but it sounded impressive. Everything Greg did seemed exciting. Maybe, she thought, it was just Greg himself.

He wandered back to the darkroom then, and Fran turned her attention to a young girl who suddenly rushed up to the counter. Breathless, she explained that her mother was driving around the block because they couldn't locate a parking place.

"The name's Bailey," she said. "You called my mother."

"Oh, yes." Because there was no money involved and the girl was in such a hurry, Fran didn't bother to open the envelope.

Alone again, she returned to the telephone list, wondering if she would reach the end of the stack before the day was over. Later, Millie walked in.

"I never dreamed it was lunch time already!" Fran exclaimed as she glanced at the clock. "The morning just zoomed by!"

She went back to the portrait room and told Mrs. Prince that she was leaving. "Fine, dear! I'm glad you're going early. As soon as you come back, I have to go home for the day."

As they walked up the street, Fran noticed that her friend was wearing her best suit—the brown wool with fur trim. "Millie, what's the occasion?"

"I'm going uptown with Pete and Betsy Parker—and Joe," she said. "A movie and a stroll through the library. Don't laugh—that's Betsy's idea. She has some strange assignment in sociology. Then hamburgers, I guess."

Fran found herself forcing a smile as if she were posing in front of Mr. Prince's camera. "It sounds fun."

"I wish you were going, Fran." Millie sounded wistful. "Now that I'm dating Pete, and he and Joe get along, well, it's such a shame that you and I can't double-date. Betsy's all right, but it's not the same."

Fran stared ahead. "Millie, if you don't mind, I'd rather you didn't mention Joe and Betsy again. He can take her, or anyone he likes, anywhere he wants to. And if you don't stop trying to push me at Joe, I—I'll stop seeing you!" She had never been so curt with Millie, but she couldn't help it now.

Millie walked silently for a moment. Then, turning into the sandwich shop, she gave a little shrug. "If that's the way you want it, Fran. I was just trying to be your friend."

Fran laughed softly, trying to smooth it over. "Well, then, stop stabbing me in the heart."

As soon as Fran returned from lunch, she found the young girl she had waited on a short time before standing at the counter with another woman and Mrs. Prince.

"Fran." Mrs. Prince looked at her anxiously. "This is Mrs. Bailey. Her daughter came in for pictures a while ago, but you didn't give her all of them."

"Oh, dear!" Fran tried to smile. "I—I don't understand."

"Honey," the woman was explaining, "you gave my daughter my proofs, but not hers. We both had pictures made that day."

Fran glanced at Mrs. Prince, dreading the rebuke that she expected to find in her expression, but her employer was rummaging through the proofs scattered about the counter. "They should be right here, Mrs. Bailey," Mrs. Prince declared. "Greg made these last night, and Fran has been calling the customers. I'm sorry if this has inconvenienced you, but it was a simple oversight. Here—they weren't hooked together, so they got lost in the shuffle." She handed over the daughter's proofs, and the pair left, smiling.

Fran swallowed hard as she turned to Mrs. Prince. "I'm sorry. I should have gone through those and compared the names before I started calling, or at least lined them up alphabetically. But I just followed Greg's directions and started calling customers without stopping to think."

Mrs. Prince patted Fran's arm. "You're doing splendidly. Don't let one small mistake discourage you. You can't learn this business in one short week, and we don't expect you to. Even after you're familiar with all of it, you'll still make mistakes. *We* do!" The woman's assurance warmed Fran. Yet, deep down, she was disappointed in herself. She wanted so much to be efficient all the time.

She forgot the struggles of the day, however, once Mr. Prince handed her a check at closing time. A week's pay! Before she had adjusted to that thrill, Greg insisted on driving her home in the studio station wagon.

With an impish smile, he told her, "If we deliver pictures, we should certainly deliver our prized receptionist to her door."

Driving toward Sandy Lane, Greg bemoaned the Statham wedding that was scheduled for eight o'clock. "Thank goodness, the couple getting married just before them have a cousin who's a camera bug. One wedding per Saturday night is enough for me."

Still in a daze from the special attention, Fran confessed, "I wish I could go along sometime and watch. Those weddings sound so exciting!"

Greg seemed pleased. "I think that could be arranged, Fran. I could use some help on these blow-outs. A woman's touch makes such a difference. Photographers are not too keen about nosegays that droop, or hems that don't drape, not to mention all the heads that tilt just before the shutter clicks."

"Would your parents let me?" Fran asked. Then, realizing how unsophisticated she must seem to a young man like Greg, she added casually, "It certainly would be an opportunity to learn more about the work."

"They'd be pleased," Greg assured her. "At least Mom would. I think she feels a little guilty that I shoot weddings and such alone when she used to go and help Dad on all his big assignments. Of course, any day now, I may have a partner. I'm trying to talk Barbara into going along. Would you mind making it a trio sometime?"

Remembering the girl with the bubbly voice, Fran smiled. "I'd love to, Greg, if you don't think Barbara would mind."

"Barbara's a peach. We go to Junior College together, you know. She types a lot of stuff for me."

As Fran walked up the steps of her porch a moment later, she thought about the art contest. It was the first time she had considered it at all since Mrs. Rogers had reminded her. She supposed that it was Greg's mention of Junior College that had brought it back to her attention.

Well, she thought, if I was as convinced of my talent as Mrs. Rogers is, I'd be anxious to win that contest and go away to study at an exclusive art school. But if a girl could meet a fellow as wonderful as Greg at a Junior College right in her home town—well, Fran told herself now, that's for me.

6

Two Dreams Come True

"Now, remember, Diane," Fran reminded her sister as they reached the corner of Dozier Drive and Maple Avenue, "hold your shoulders back, and for goodness sake, say 'Yes, ma'am!'"

Diane had been skipping along the sidewalk, but now she slowed to a dignified pace. With a toss of her golden hair, she said impatiently, "There you go, Fran—acting like a mother again. Glory, I know what to do. And if Mrs. King wants me to dance for her, I'll do my 'Nutcracker Suite' routine. OK?"

"I suppose so," Fran replied absently. She worried a little now about whether Diane would seem as talented to this dancing teacher as she had to all those women at the Woman's Club last year. But why would they have taken the time to seek Fran out and tell her how talented Diane was, if they hadn't been convinced of it? Glancing once more at her young sister, Fran realized with a start that Diane was nearly as tall as she. Oh, dear. Mrs. King may think she's too large for her age or too old to be just a beginner.

The possibility that Linda might qualify for piano lessons while Diane—whose sulking sessions could disrupt the entire household—might be turned down was too horrible to contemplate. Loretta King, Fran told herself, would have to find a place for Diane!

Dusk deepened into darkness, and the houses along the avenue were lighting up. When Diane commented on how pretty the homes were, Fran wistfully agreed. "I used to dream that someday we'd live in one. But it's just as well now. They're too close to the shopping center."

"Mrs. King's studio is another block down," Diane volunteered. "She lives on the first floor and her studio is on the second, and I'm glad I won't have far to walk every week." She whirled on the sidewalk then, her full skirt swishing around her knees. "Fran, I hope Mrs. King doesn't tell me to make 'doll hands.' "

"What makes you think she'll say that?"

"Oh, Linda's friend—you know, Brenda Sanders? Well, she takes ballet from Mrs. King, and Brenda's always showing Linda how she makes doll hands. Glory, it's so babyish!"

Just ahead, Fran spied a luminous marker with the number 2420 on the grass at the edge of the sidewalk. "Here we are," she said. There was a large sign posted against the second floor of the building. Barely visible now in the darkness, it announced "Loretta King School of Dance."

Fran hurried up the steps and rang the doorbell. She

turned, expecting her young sister to be waiting there beside her, wide-eyed and glowing. Instead, Diane was still on the sidewalk, propelling herself back to the end of it in a flurry of pirouettes.

"Diane!" Fran called in exasperation. "Hurry, I hear footsteps!" Diane sprang forward and bounded up the steps just as the door opened.

A petite young woman in a black leotard, her dark hair wound in a braid, looked at them quizzically.

"Mrs. King, I'm Fran Avery. I called—"

"Of course, the Avery girls!" Her voice was soft, melodious. "Won't you come in?"

Fran's gaze was instantly attracted to the unusual decor. There were no colors in the living room except white and gold. A gold satin sofa, flanked with white end tables, curved around a thick white rug. Gold and white lamps vied for attention with elegant gold satin draperies. Standing there against this background, like a lone stroke of black across a white canvas, was Loretta King.

The young woman seemed unaware of Fran's fascination. She led Diane over to the satin sofa. "Have you had any lessons at all, Diane?" she asked.

Without waiting for her sister to reply, Fran interrupted. "No, ma'am—none at all."

Mrs. King smiled indulgently. "I'm sure Diane can answer for herself. Tell me, dear, why do you want to take lessons?"

"Why?" Diane's eyes widened. "Glory, because I want to!" She turned to Fran, her face reddening. "Didn't you tell Mrs. King all about me, Fran, when you phoned her?"

Fran stiffened. *She's going to ruin everything by acting Jamie's age!*

Mrs. King continued before Fran could intervene. "Your sister explained that she would like to have you take lessons.

That was her reason, but I want to know yours. What does dancing mean to you?"

"It means a lot," Diane said now in a tremulous voice. She lowered her head and stared down. Fran marveled, then, because her sister's hands were lying in her lap, curled into the "doll hands" that she loathed.

It was obvious that Mrs. King noticed the gesture, too, for she reached over and touched Diane's arm. "You've said enough. Come. I'll show you my studio, and you can show me the other things you've taught yourself."

As Mrs. King led them up the stairs to the second floor, Diane beamed back at Fran as if to say: "I'm fine. I can take it from here."

Somewhat relieved, Fran followed the pair into a huge room that was bare except for a large piano in the corner beside the door. A wooden rail that Mrs. King called the "barre" ran along one wall, and covering the opposite wall was an immense mirror.

There were no chairs, so Fran leaned against the wall beside the door. Mrs. King sat down at the piano and began to play chords.

"Do you know the five positions, Diane?"

"Yes, ma'am!" she exclaimed. "For the hands and feet. And I made up some dances."

"I see." The dance teacher was watching Diane intently now. "Let your movements blend and flow, blend and flow."

Diane seemed not to hear. She was standing immobile, staring into the mirror at her own reflection. "Glory, now I can watch myself and see how gracefully I dance, can't I?"

Mrs. King's reply was firm. "The purpose, Diane, is to watch for our mistakes, so we can improve our form."

"Yes, ma'am. I—I guess so."

The teacher began to play a lilting melody, and Diane's hands and feet, moving simultaneously and in rhythm, proceeded through the five basic ballet positions.

Fran stood rigidly, trying not to think how much her pretty blond sister resembled a mechanical doll. *Why doesn't she show Mrs. King how graceful she really can be?*

It was soon apparent that Mrs. King was familiar with the tension of young beginners. She continued to play, over and over, until Diane relaxed. She eventually began to perform a routine that she had created herself after watching ballet dancing on TV and in the movies. With the teacher supplying a thread of melody, Diane wove an intricate pattern of ballet movements—that included arabesques and pliés and ended in the more difficult tour jeté.

While Fran waited almost breathlessly, Mrs. King got up slowly and walked around the piano and paused. She was frowning as if in deep thought. "Fran," she began quietly, "I simply can't put Diane in a beginners' class. She's older than any of my beginners, and she's so much larger."

Diane rushed over, with a stricken expression. "You aren't going to teach me?"

Mrs. King slipped an arm around her affectionately. "Of course, dear, but I think you have far too much talent to be wasted in a group. You deserve private lessons."

"Private lessons?" Fran blurted. Until then, she hadn't considered such a possibility. "But aren't they awfully expensive?"

"Yes," Mrs. King replied. "About twice the price of group lessons. But a talented child can progress three or four times faster." She folded her arms as she added, "I teach only talented children privately, Fran. I make no exceptions for mothers who *think* that their children deserve such coaching."

Fran searched her sister's face. She'd never seen her so

distressed. "I'm not sure I can afford private lessons. You see—" Before she began her tale of financial woe, Fran suddenly realized how grateful she should be that this woman felt that Diane warranted such exclusive attention. She knew now that Diane really had talent and that all her struggles wouldn't be in vain. "I'll have to think about it," she said.

Fran couldn't bear to look at Diane because she couldn't trust her own emotions just then. She heard Mrs. King speaking. "My dear, you must consider the unusual circumstances involved and what's best for Diane. She would feel awkward in a class with younger, smaller girls. Yet, she'd have a miserable time trying to keep up with my advanced girls, the ones around her own age."

It was Diane who spoke up first, impatiently. "Mrs. King, don't you have some other girl about my age who's starting lessons late the way I am?"

Mrs. King smiled. "I was getting around to that. I do know of such a girl. She's thirteen and small for her age. Her mother is rather peeved because I haven't agreed to teach her privately. She does have some talent, but I personally feel that the child doesn't want to work as hard as her mother expects her to. Now, Fran, if this mother and daughter are agreeable, would you consider semi-private lessons? I don't like such classes because they cause unnecessary competition, but I do make exceptions. They would cost very little more than class lessons, yet Diane would learn so much more."

Mrs. King turned to Diane now. "You'd have to be patient, dear, if your partner doesn't grasp something as quickly as you might."

Diane brightened. "Glory, I'd be so patient, you'd never recognize me! Mrs. King, please make that lady agreeable!"

Fran laughed at Diane's enthusiasm, and Loretta King

joined in with a merriment that made her seem younger than before.

"Mrs. King," Fran said as they were leaving, "I don't know how to thank you for helping us like this. You'll call us when it's definite?"

"It's practically certain now. They're just as anxious to begin lessons as Diane is. Oh, yes, the lessons will be on Thursdays at four-thirty. It's the only spot I have left."

On the way home, while Diane chattered beside her, Fran's thoughts were whirling ahead. Her salary would easily afford Diane her semi-private lessons and Linda her piano lessons. But there was so much more she hoped to buy. So many more expenses were involved. She thought of the car, sitting in the garage. Well, she told herself, if they waited long enough, they could auction it off as an antique.

Diane greeted the family, assembled in the living room, with a graceful arabesque.

"Is she gonna teach you?" Linda cried as she jumped up from the sofa. "Real lessons?"

"Real lessons!" Diane exclaimed joyously. "Semi-private lessons because I'm so talented!" Soon she'd told it all in a torrent of words. "I get to warm up at the barre and wear real ballet shoes. And there's a big mirror, longer than our whole living room, so I can watch myself!"

"That's all Diane does at home, Sis," Jamie pointed out. "You gonna pay money for her to see herself in a mirror?"

Too contented to be ruffled, Diane chuckled. "You just wait, Jamie. You'll pay lots of money to watch me some day after I'm a famous ballerina." She punctuated her remark with an energetic tour jeté.

Fran sank into a tired heap on the sofa. She looked over at her mother, who was mending a loose zipper on one of

Linda's skirts. "Did you find out anything about Linda's lessons?"

Mrs. Avery nodded. "Yes. Mrs. Hart and I had quite a conversation. I think she labeled me a bad mother because I can't march right out and buy Linda a fine, new piano. I've noticed that women who've never worked outside the home have no idea how hard it is to make a living for a family!"

Fran stared at her mother. "She wants Linda to have a new piano?"

"Oh, she didn't insist," her mother replied, "she just advised. Relax, dear, and I'll explain, but I can't in one breath as Diane does! First, I told her that our church pianist, who had recommended her, insists that Linda has a strong musical talent. But when I finally admitted that the only piano we have is a beat-up thing that I've stored here in the girls' bedroom for a friend, well—she grew rather cool. In a nice way, she informed me that it would impede Linda's progress to practice on such an old piano. She agreed that a good tuning job would help. But then she made a speech about how, if I was truly interested in Linda's talent, I'd have only the best! Believe me, I nearly told her off!"

"Mother," Fran interrupted, "that's practically what Mrs. King told me." She related the conversation with the dancing teacher. "Do you suppose they tell that to everyone just so they'll make more money, or something?"

Mrs. Avery shook her head. "Now, what would Mrs. Hart gain if Linda did have a new piano? Except," she added, "a better pupil. I'm sure that's all Mrs. King wants. They're just two conscientious teachers, and we should be grateful for that."

Fran leaned back against the sofa. "That's all we can afford to do now, Mother," she said miserably. "Be grateful." She kicked off her shoes. "Well, there goes all my generosity. I wouldn't dream of giving Diane lessons if

Linda can't have any, and I certainly can't afford a new piano!"

"Oh, Fran," her mother exclaimed, "I'm not finished. She gave me the names of several piano tuners, so I can choose one. But she suggested that we keep searching the want ads until we find someone with a newer piano who'll allow the use of it in exchange for storing it here."

"Then Linda can take lessons?" Fran gasped.

"Yes. She can start Saturday morning if you like."

"Oh, Mother!" Fran began to laugh, but her laughter was mixed with tears of relief. "Keeping me in suspense all that time!"

Mrs. Avery chuckled amiably. "You know me well enough by now to know that I get the worst over first. Of course, it's up to you—you're the one paying for it. And if we can't find a piano to store, we may have to buy another one, a second-hand one that's not quite so decrepit."

Linda moved over to Fran and clutched her hand. "Please, Sis, you promised! You know you did!"

Oh, dear. Fran felt quivery inside from the strain of the evening. It was costing so much more than she had imagined, but she had made this decision, and she had promised her sisters. Besides, the hardest part—getting a job—was behind her.

Fran looked at the girls sternly now. "I'll agree, but on one condition. If you two don't practice and keep up your chores, the lessons are over! If you want to find out how much I mean that, just stop doing your part. Then, I'll have to quit my job. And no job, no lessons. As for the piano, though, we'll worry about that later. One problem at a time, please."

7

A New Friend

Soup was on the menu, Fran decided, as she bounded down the stairs toward the lunchroom. She had suffered hunger pangs all during her third-period class, and now the hearty aroma of tomatoes, peas, and beef simmering together reminded her sharply that she hadn't eaten all her breakfast that morning.

It had been Diane's fault, Fran reflected now. A brief ten minutes before the time Fran usually left for school, Diane had concluded that her hair was a frizzy mop. All Fran's efforts to convince her sister that her golden hair hanging loose around her shoulders was quite becoming failed to impress Diane. To prove how serious she considered the crisis, Diane had thrown her hairbrush across the bedroom.

"Glory, Fran!" she exclaimed, suddenly meek, "I'm sorry! I—I forgot, Fran. You won't stop my lessons, will you?" She whirled around and rushed over to retrieve the brush.

More anxious to leave for school than angry, Fran told her, "We'll forget it this time, Diane. But you've got to control your temper and stop punishing the rest of us just because your hair or your dress or whatever it is that you imagine isn't perfect annoys you!"

Then, at Diane's request, Fran had put her sister's hair back in its familiar pony-tail style, leaving herself only enough time to make one sandwich for her lunch.

Fran pushed away the memory now, telling herself that she had enough problems of her own this week without worrying about Diane's temperament. There was a theme due in Lit 3, and she hadn't even begun it yet.

"Fran!" Millie was calling to her across the confusion of students pushing into the school cafeteria. "Hurry—the cheerleaders practice!"

Obediently, Fran quickened her pace, but her heartbeats slowed. Not another practice session, she thought miserably. Would football and all that went with it ever be over?

V-i-c-t-o-r-y! *That's our goal for Waverly High!*
Rah! Rah! Rah, Rah, Rah! Waverly's got it on the ball!

The silly shouts had roared up through the open windows to distract her in class. They'd followed her down the corridors and haunted her in study hall. Why, she wondered, should football season annoy me? She'd always been interested in the games and gleefully joined in the cheers. Just because she wouldn't have time for the games shouldn't make any difference!

"C'mon," Millie urged. "My soup's getting cold!"

"I'm sorry, Millie. You really shouldn't have waited for me. You see, I won't have time to watch the practice, anyway."

They had reached the end of the table where Millie had used her lunch tray and a pile of books to reserve two spaces opposite one another. She looked up, frowning. "Fran, you're not serious!"

Fran sat down, tore into her lunch sack, and took the carton of milk Millie had bought for her. "Look, Millie, I really must do some research in the library for that lit theme." She tried to impress her friend with her busy schedule, but even as she talked, she felt, deep down, as if she were trying to convince herself that she wasn't really avoiding the practice session.

Millie shrugged and began salting her soup. "Have it your way, Fran, but I still think you're foolish. You see what that job has already done? You've never missed a cheerleader practice with me, and you've never been behind on a theme before!"

Fran lifted her chin. "Well, I can't have everything, you know. Why should I get all excited, when I won't be going to the games, anyway?"

"That's all the more reason that you should be interested, Fran. You don't want everyone to think you've lost your school spirit!"

Fran stopped sipping her milk. "And what's wrong with my school spirit?" she demanded. "Just because I don't get out there and yell!"

"Don't be so touchy, Fran," Millie whispered. "And lower your voice. We're being watched."

Fran felt her face stinging. Others were staring at them.

Almost immediately, Laura Maynard and Kit Kellogg were standing there beside them. "Ready, girls?" Laura smiled impishly, pushing up the sleeves of her newest cashmere sweater.

"Fran's not going," Milllie announced, as if it were a disaster.

"What a shame!" Laura exclaimed. "The team's showing off their new uniforms. They've even erected a platform—"

"That's for the rally this afternoon," Kit spoke up quickly. "They're just getting things ready now."

"Well," Laura replied with a dramatic note of pity, "Fran will miss that, too, won't she? She works in the afternoons now."

Fran was certain her face was flaming, but her voice was cool. "I'm flattered that you remembered."

"I think Fran's pretty smart," Kit declared. "If I weren't so lazy, I'd get myself a job. Saturdays get so boring at home."

A group of seniors passed, luring Laura and Kit to join them. Millie soon joined the mass exodus to the ball field, and Fran realized that she and one small group, still eating, were the only students left in the lunchroom.

I don't care, she thought defensively. Let them think I've lost my school spirit. I can't hold a job and go to pep rallies and games and keep up with my studies, too.

Passing through the corridors later, she noticed that some classes were still in session and that other students were concentrating on their studies, oblivious to the commotion outside. She slipped into the silent depths of the library and hid in the classic literature section. After she'd collected her thoughts and organized her notes, she looked up several items in the catalogue files. Then she got the necessary books.

She had replaced the last book on the shelf when the fifth-period bell buzzed out in the hall. As she reached sociology class, a girl stepped out from the doorway and handed her a note. "You are Fran Avery, aren't you?" she asked.

"Why, yes!" Fran watched, bewildered, as the girl disappeared up the stairs. Then she unfolded the slip of paper. "Fran," the note read, "I must talk to you. Please come to my room after school." It was signed "Mrs. Mason."

Fran wondered now what Mrs. Mason could possibly want with her. Laura Maynard was supposed to have made the explanations. But Fran rushed downstairs after the final bell and went into room 114.

Mrs. Mason sat at her desk, fidgeting with a black velvet beret that perched atop the thick hair that she had dyed henna-red this year. She pointed to a chair.

"Now, Fran, what's this I hear about your dropping out of the club and working after school? And why haven't you told me?"

"Mrs. Mason," Fran began in astonishment, "Laura told me she would tell you about my job and all. I—well, I didn't think it mattered that much, my being in the Dramatic Club or not."

The teacher dabbed on a touch of lipstick. "It mattered to me, my dear! You were the only dependable Girl Friday I had last year. Most of the girls want to play the leading role. Fran, could you possibly fit the club into your schedule? I've finally got things in shape early enough to do a mystery for Hallowe'en. But I'm desperate for another helper."

Mrs. Mason gave Fran a solemn, searching look. "Fran, my dear, if I forgot to tell you last year how helpful you were, please forgive me. I was so pleased when you signed up last spring."

Fran swallowed hard. "I'm sorry, Mrs. Mason. I really intended to be in the club this year, when I signed up last May, but circumstances— Well, I just had to take this job."

The teacher smiled wryly. "Well, you don't seem to be spending it all on yourself. Must be financial troubles." Before Fran could adjust to the blunt remark, Mrs. Mason added, "I'm an old busybody, Fran! You aren't obligated to help the club, even if you don't have a job."

Mrs. Mason stood up quickly and, with a broad smile, extended a hand. Fran took it hesitantly and stammered out another apology before she turned away. When she reached the doorway, she called back, "I hope the club has a wonderful year, Mrs. Mason!"

The September sun was still warm on her face, but there were enough leaves stirring along the sidewalk to warn Fran that autumn was practically there.

Instead of setting her usual brisk pace toward the shopping center, Fran plodded today, heavy with a sense of guilt. When she had debated the pros and cons of a part-time job, she had never imagined there would be such strange reactions to her decision. Why, her friends treated her as if she'd betrayed them for a few pieces of silver! When she reached the traffic light at Maple Avenue, three blocks from the studio, Fran shifted her books and heaved a long, weary sigh.

"It couldn't be all that bad!" someone spoke from behind.

Startled, Fran spun around to identify the deep, masculine voice. Although the face looked familiar, she failed to recognize the lean, black-haired boy who was grinning at her.

Then, she remembered. "You're that new boy in Lit 3!" she exclaimed. "Oh, dear. Your name's Watson?"

"Watts," he replied, crossing the street beside her now. "Chris Watts. And you're Fran Avery. You sit on the second seat of the front row, while I sit on the last seat of the last row. You'd think a high school teacher could be more original than that. If he'd spell Waverly on the first row, for instance, then you'd be sitting right behind me!'"

Fran couldn't hold back her laughter. "So that's what you're daydreaming about when Mr. DeLong calls on you in class!"

"That," he said, "and other vital things like fishing and bowling and pretty girls—which brings me back to the present. I've been trying to catch up with you all week. Some days I see you pass the physics lab before I leave. Most of the time I miss you altogether until I pass Prince's Studio and see you inside."

Fran looked at him carefully, then. "You visit the shopping center every day? Why?"

"I work down here, dear girl. My dad bought that sporting-goods store at the end of the block. Haven't you noticed the neon sign that's already on the blink: *atts Sporting Goods*? Well, 'atts us! I'll be glad when the repairmen get around to us. We get ribbed a lot."

Fran found herself giggling now. "It's wonderful to meet you, Chris. I should have introduced myself before and welcomed you to Waverly High, but the community's been growing so fast that it's hard to get around to all the new ones. You'll learn to like it here, I'm sure."

"I like it already," he admitted. "There's a lot of school spirit, and it's good for business, especially our business. Dad's stocking batons and uniforms and pennants—all to fill the needs of Waverly High."

As he talked, Fran realized how similar their situations were. Chris was a senior, but he spent his afternoons working in his father's store. When she mentioned this to him, he insisted that he had no choice. "I have to work, Fran, because Dad can't afford to hire extra help yet. But the truth is, I enjoy it. One afternoon at the store is more fun than two of those pep rallies!"

"My hero!" Fran teased. "Really, Chris, it's wonderful to meet someone who is honest enough to admit that there are other things in life besides football games. Some of my friends think I'm being a martyr. I guess I'll never convince them that I *like* my job."

"And what do you care? You can't please everyone, Fran, so just please your own conscience. You know, as much as I like it, I'm not sure I'd help Dad so much if he didn't pay me something for my efforts, but I've had guys kid me for taking money from my own father. What's so criminal about that? He'd have to pay someone, wouldn't he, so why not me?"

The traffic light blinked green, and the two crossed Maple Avenue, chatting pleasantly as they neared Prince's Studio. At the doorway, Chris waved good-by and headed down the street.

Fran pushed open the glass door and went inside, her heart thudding happily. She had almost concluded that the day was a dismal failure until Chris had come along and made her realize that she was a free agent. Of course, she told herself now, it really doesn't matter what others think my motives are, as long as I know in my heart that I'm right. It came to her then that Chris, in a way, was very much like Greg.

8

Fran Tries to Please

Fran dabbed another blob of green water-color paint on the thirsty white paper and brushed it across the bottom of the painting in wide, bold strokes. She added another strip of darker green under the lighter area, then stopped and studied the effect.

It's awful, she thought. It's really awful! She glanced toward the front of the room, at the still-life arrangement that Mrs. Rogers had set up for the class to sketch during today's double-lab period. On the table she had placed a white ceramic bowl filled with stubby ferns that peeked over the brim. Beside it was a luscious red apple. Behind these, she had put a large, oval-shaped pottery tray in a rich chartreuse color. Fran had painted all sorts of similar arrangements during art classes for two years now, but none of the results had disappointed her quite so much.

Studying the painting objectively, Fran saw clearly that the tray was out of proportion to the other objects. She bit her lip in utter frustration. She'd spent an hour on the picture, and now she was ashamed to have anyone see it. It wouldn't matter so much, she thought, if she hadn't planned to send this very painting to that national art contest.

Fran had finally resigned herself to the inevitable. Mrs. Rogers had made that contest a personal crusade. Several times a week she inquired if Fran was working on anything new. So, this afternoon, faced with a double-lab and another still-life arrangement, she'd made a hasty decision that seemed a solution to everything. She would use her class projects as entries in the contest.

Fran stiffened as she sensed someone looking over her shoulder. She disliked having anyone hover over her while she painted, and Mrs. Rogers, of all people, was the worst offender.

"Fran—" The teacher's voice was low. "You're out of proportion. The tray is much too large. You're not following my advice, dear. Block out every object before you splash on paint."

"I did," Fran explained, "in my mind, but it didn't work. I guess I was trying to save time. Mrs. Rogers," Fran went on, "I was hoping to use some of my class projects and enter them in the contest—just the good ones, of course."

"Fine! But it won't be easy. With only one double period each week, it will be difficult to complete any water-color pieces with quality. Of course, you should also hand in work in other media—charcoal sketches, pastel, even some block prints."

"I was hoping to finish about two paintings a week and

use a few I've already done—" Her words trailed off as she watched the teacher's reaction.

"My dear girl," Mrs. Rogers said, with an exasperation that she usually reserved for students who left paint jars uncapped and brushes lying about, "I will not allow you to enter shoddy work, or work you did last year. Fran, you must strive for the very best you can do."

Fran felt tears creeping into her eyes. "Well," she said feebly, "I guess there's no use in my trying, because I won't have time to do my very best."

After the words were said, Fran regretted them. Mrs. Rogers moved on, wordlessly, to the next student. Fran stared at her drawing board, pretending great interest in her work. She wondered miserably how one part-time job could cause her so many humiliating moments.

Well, she consoled herself now, she didn't care about the contest. She was certain that her art work hadn't a glimmer of a chance among all that competition, but she did want to keep peace with Mrs. Rogers.

Calmly, then, Fran wadded up the painting and discarded it. She pulled a clean, white sheet out of her art folder. This time she intended to block out every object with care before she dipped into paint. She had barely begun when the bell rang.

Scooping up her brushes and paint boxes, Fran told herself that she would make up for today, perhaps tomorrow. While Fran crowded at the wash basins with other students, Mrs. Rogers approached, reminding a pupil to clear off a near-by work table.

When she reached Fran, she spoke in a low, confidential tone. "You're in a hurry, so I'll be brief. I've probably given you the impression that I'm dictatorial, but I'm not. I simply feel that it's my duty to encourage talent."

The room was almost empty now, and Fran stood alone at

the basin, wiping her brushes slowly, yearning to look at the clock, while Mrs. Rogers went on, "Now, Fran, I have several promising students, but you're blessed with such an abundance of ability that—well, I suppose I'm trying to say that to whom much is given, from them much is expected. Fran, those of us who have been blessed with talent must develop it. We owe it to ourselves and to others. But it demands a price—hard work and sacrifice. In your circumstances, you'll have to forego a lot of social life. For instance, giving up one party would give you enough time to paint a still-life. Do you understand?"

Fran looked back at Mrs. Rogers incredulously. What, she wanted to ask, didn't require hard work and sacrifice? And why weren't those who were blessed with talent also blessed with the time and money to develop it? She thought of all the hours they had spent trying to locate a piano worthy of Linda's fine talent.

"Mrs. Rogers," Fran said unsteadily, "I've already given up most of my social life. And I appreciate your interest, but I—I can't promise that I'll come up with a lot of new paintings. I'll just do the best I can."

Shortly after five, Chris Watts strolled into the photography studio. He waited at the end of the counter while the customers thinned out.

"Where were you today?" Fran finally asked. "I was late leaving art, so I probably just missed you."

Chris was grinning. "I had other fish to fry, my girl! You're now looking at a new car owner. Well, not a *new* car, just a new owner. Dad promised me one my senior year, so now I won't have to beg the station wagon anymore." His voice lowered. "Fran, you'll be my first passenger, if you'll let me drive you home!"

"I'm flattered," she teased. "And your offer couldn't be

more convenient. Greg usually drives me home after work, but today he's out on assignment. I'll try to leave promptly at six-thirty."

"But who is he, Fran?" Diane persisted as she followed Fran out to the kitchen.

Grabbing up an apron, Fran tied it over her skirt, sniffing the fragrant aroma of a chuck roast. "Did you put it on as soon as you got home from school, Diane?" she asked.

"Yes, and I turned it over and over. But who *is* that boy who brought you home?"

"His name is Chris Watts," Fran replied. She peered into the oven at the meat browning amid potatoes and onions. Turning away, she realized that her young sister was still waiting for an explanation.

"Look, Diane, he just moved to Waverly this summer, so all I know is that he's a senior and his father now runs that sporting-goods store across from Draper's."

Diane sighed dramatically. "Well, if I were you, I'd want to know more about him. He sure is good looking. What color are his eyes?"

Fran paused. "I really haven't noticed. I think they're blue."

"Glory, a boy drives you home, and you don't know what color his eyes are?"

"Look, Mata Hari, Chris and I sit at opposite ends of the room in Lit 3. Frankly, I've been too busy to notice what color my own eyes are!"

Diane tossed her pony tail impishly. "Yeah—you didn't even put on fresh lipstick."

"I know. Just before time to leave, there was a phone call. Some woman was all upset because the photographer she had hired to take pictures at a big club banquet didn't show up. She knows Mrs. Prince, and she wanted to ask her if she could sue that photographer! Well, Mr. Prince and Greg were busy, so finally I gave her Mrs. Prince's number at home. I hated to bother her, but the woman was so persistent."

Diane was setting plates around the table now. "Well, could they?" Her eyes were bright with curiosity. "Could that lady sue that man?"

"I really don't know," Fran admitted. "The question hasn't come up before. But I don't see how she could unless the agreement was in writing or something. I mean, how could she prove that she had called that particular photographer or that she'd told him the correct date? Chris said a lot of times it depends on the lawyer who handles the case."

"Wouldn't it be horrible?" Diane said earnestly. "If you were getting married and wanted some pretty pictures and the man didn't even show up? How would you ever show anybody what a beautiful bride you were? I sure hope that doesn't happen to me!"

"Well," Fran replied with a chuckle, "if you expect to be a bride someday, you'd better learn to be a housewife. So try setting the table for a meal, honey. Right now it looks like a jigsaw puzzle."

9

Betsy's Party

"Hey, Fran, here comes Joe!" Linda yelled out the kitchen window. "He's walking around to the back yard right now! Fran?"

"I heard you, Linda," Fran replied. "The whole neighborhood heard you!"

Sprawled on an old quilt in the back yard, Fran glanced in dismay at her faded pedal pushers. Then she remembered her hair and the curlers jutting out all over her head. Oh, dear! But it was too late to escape. Joe strode toward her, clad in fresh Levis and a white sport shirt, with his copper-colored hair blazing above.

"So this is the poor working class!" he teased, standing

over her. "How's this for beautiful weather?" he added, stretching lazily. "Seventy-five degrees in the last week of October."

"It's been wonderful," Fran declared, pushing herself to a sitting position. "But where did you come from? Last I heard, you were all tied up with out-of-town relatives." She began peeling curlers out of her hair.

"They changed their plans," he said, watching her in fascination.

"No cracks about all the glamour," Fran warned him. "I'm making myself beautiful for a very special date tonight."

"So, I heard." Joe lowered his husky frame until he was sitting on the grass beside the quilt, his brown eyes level with hers. "How special is it? A party?"

"No. Why?" she asked guardedly. For weeks now, she had been dreading an occasion when she and Chris and Joe would be together, and she sensed that this question concerned just that.

"Oh, Betsy's having some of the gang over after Youth League tonight. Since Chris belongs to it, I thought you two might be going. Millie and Pete will be there, you know."

"I know. I've been to League with Chris once before and with Millie, too. Chris mentioned it, and I'd like to go, but I can't stay out so late." She didn't add that she really dreaded competing with Betsy Parker's lavish hair-do's and extravagant dresses. "Besides," she pointed out, "Betsy wouldn't be expecting us."

"Asking you was my idea," Joe said, "though Betsy did tell me to invite a few of my friends. You know, the more the merrier."

"How convenient for you," Fran retorted, astonished at the sarcasm shadowing her words. Now, why, she wondered, should Joe frustrate me like this? But as Joe elaborated on the party and Betsy's crowd, Fran knew that she was afflicted with a mild case of jealousy. Lately, whenever she'd heard their names linked or seen their hands clasped in the hall, she'd felt a knot tighten in her stomach. She'd soothed her wounded ego by reminding herself that she had a job, her own friends, including a handsome new senior named Chris, so why should she care?

She forced herself to smile graciously now. "Thanks, Joe, for inviting us. It really does sound like fun."

Moments later, when Joe's car chugged away in the distance, Fran went into the house, balancing the box of curlers in one hand and carrying the quilt with the other. She almost collided with Diane in the kitchen doorway. "Glory," Diane exclaimed, "I thought you'd never come back inside! You're always bragging about being so busy, but you sure do loaf a lot!"

"*Loaf?*" Fran snapped. "I've been out there curling my hair and doing my nails and enjoying what will probably be the last sunny day for months. I won't list all the things I did after we got home from church!" Walking past her sister, Fran asked, "Where's Mother?"

"She went up to Mrs. Brown's," Diane replied in a hurt tone. "She took that material she bought her on sale. Jamie went, too."

In her room, Fran shoved the box of curlers in a drawer of her dresser and sat down before the mirror. She put her face in her hands and squeezed her eyes shut to try to hold back the tears. I shouldn't have been cross with her. I can't expect Diane to control her temper if *I* can't do it. But it was all so discouraging. No matter how many small chores she assigned to the children, there were still dozens that only Fran and her mother could do. And no matter how well she organized her hours at home, those twenty-four hours she gave to the studio took a chunk of time out of her life that no amount of efficiency could overcome. And now, she told herself, Diane comes along and makes me feel guilty because I took a break.

Fran gathered up her clothes and went across the hall to the bathroom. Tucking her curls securely under a plastic shower cap, she let the water rush over her full force. To herself she could admit that she would like to spend an evening with a crowd for a change, even at Betsy's house. Much as she enjoyed Chris's company, there really wasn't much they could do on Sunday evenings. Besides, with Millie there tonight, Betsy wouldn't seem so overpowering.

When Fran returned to her dressing table, Linda was perched on its bench, puffing clouds of powder on her small, solemn face. "Let me go with you, Fran. I never get to go anywhere!"

"Oh, no?" Fran challenged teasingly. "Just to school and piano lessons and all over the neighborhood to play." She persuaded her to give up the bench. "And, sweetie, please don't play with my make-up anymore. It's so expensive. I have to make it last for ages and ages."

Unperturbed, Linda went on, "Diane says she's gonna use mascara when she's seventeen."

"It wouldn't surprise me," Fran said with a chuckle. She rummaged around in a drawer until she found an old tube of lipstick. "Here, Linda, you can play lady with this." Linda skipped beaming out of the room.

Fran applied a sheer film of powder over her freshly-scrubbed face. As she studied her own irregular features, she mused over Millie's explanation of Betsy's dark, delicate beauty. "She does it with mirrors, honey. Lots of them."

In the kitchen, Fran protected her freshly pressed blue sheath dress with an apron and deftly put together a snack of sandwiches. Then she called to the children to come and eat.

Her mother returned soon after, and Fran asked, "Mother, would you mind keeping the children here in the kitchen until Chris and I leave? Diane's practically got us engaged."

When the doorbell rang, Fran answered. "Hi!" she said.

Chris grinned approvingly at her appearance. "Wow! Special occasion?"

"Could be," Fran teased. "We were invited to a party, if you'd like to go." Leading him over to the sofa, she sat beside him and quickly explained.

Chris shrugged. "Why not? I think it was rather clever of Joe to include us. But I've been trying to place Betsy Parker. The name clicks somehow—"

Fran almost laughed aloud. Here she had been dreading the *femme fatale*, and Chris couldn't even remember Betsy. "She's the gorgeous brunette. That time we went to League together, she wore a flaming red suit."

"Oh!" Chris brightened. "The butterfly!"

"Now, why did you call her that?"

"Because she flits from one person to another," he replied simply. "She's pretty all right, but I prefer a girl who isn't always trying to impress everyone."

"Like me," Fran inserted impishly, "impressing no one!"

"Like you," Chris agreed, clutching her hand suddenly. Fran grew uncomfortable under Chris's tender gaze. She didn't want him to be *this* fond of her. She just wanted to be friends.

"We'd better go," she said lightly, easing her hand from his. "I'll get my jacket. It's getting cool again."

When she returned, Chris was surrounded by noisy children. She heard him promising to take them to the zoo. "Oh, Chris, I leave you for one minute, and they wring a promise out of you!"

He was grinning. "It was my idea!"

Fran's mother appeared, flustered and apologizing for the

children. As Fran went out to the car with Chris, she said, "I really don't know why we should apologize for these kids because you should feel flattered, Chris. They don't usually take to strangers so quickly."

"Stranger! As often as I've been to your house in the past month?"

He shut the door on her side, then went around and slid under the steering wheel.

"Chris," Fran said quietly, "I didn't mean it that way. I guess it's Joe's fault. He spoiled them. When he first started driving, he took them around a lot to get ice cream or something. Now they think that all my dates are supposed to treat them."

After a pause, Chris said, "Did you and Joe go steady for a long time?"

Fran felt her face smarting. She'd given Chris the wrong impression. "Look—" She paused and then rushed the words out before she considered whether or not she should, "I've never really dated Joe. I mean, real dates. He's been a neighbor so long that he's like a member of the family."

Fran sat stiffly on a folding chair beside Chris in a corner of the spacious Parker living room, thinking that the evening wasn't turning out at all as she had expected. It wasn't Betsy's fault. Fran had discovered that Betsy Parker was as gracious a hostess as she was beautiful.

I guess I'm just a misfit, Fran told herself now, as the conversation droned on about the Hallowe'en play that the Dramatic Club had presented the evening before. Laura Maynard and Kit Kellogg and others in the cast were sharing bits of onstage and offstage gossip with those who had been in the audience. Fran felt as if she was being pushed, word by word, into the dark, empty wings.

Abruptly, Betsy turned toward Fran and Chris and

gasped, "How rude of us! We've been discussing the play, and suddenly I realized that you two weren't even there. What a shame!"

"I had to help my dad," Chris explained casually. "But if you want to hold a command performance here, we'll watch! Fran—well, she was much too busy."

"Terribly." Fran spoke up, forcing gaiety into her words. "I spent most of the week getting off entries in an art contest, so I was whirling yesterday, trying to catch up."

"That's right!" Betsy cooed now. "You're the artist!" She tilted her dark head demurely. "You're so smart and talented, Fran. You make a girl like me feel so—well, unambitious!"

"This was Mrs. Rogers' idea," Fran told them. "I really don't expect even an honorable mention."

Presently, when Betsy got up to serve refreshments, Millie insisted that she and Fran would help. "I want to talk to you," she whispered to Fran as they withdrew from the others. There was no chance for a private conversation, though, until they were carrying sandwich trays from the kitchen through the dining room and on to the living room. While Betsy walked ahead of them with paper plates and napkins, Millie detained Fran long enough to convey the idea that she was disappointed in her.

"Fran, when will you learn that you have to make a boy jealous to make him notice you? You have a perfect opportunity tonight with Chris here."

"But I don't want to make Joe or anyone jealous!" Fran exclaimed. "Really, I wouldn't know how."

"Well, you're off to a grand start. Joe's been watching you all evening."

"Oh, Millie," Fran flared, "can't you leave me alone? You nag me to come to these parties, and now you want to turn this one into a—a battleground. Look, if Joe likes Betsy, that's his business."

Millie's gray eyes clouded. "Fran, you've changed. I can't explain it, but you have—even toward me."

"Forgive me, Millie. I guess I'm just bushed." Fran said it gently. Millie shrugged, then, as if the issue wasn't important.

The two carried the sandwiches on into the living room. There Betsy confronted Fran. "Would you help me with the punch?" she asked, taking the tray from Fran and giving it to Laura Maynard to pass.

Surprised, Fran stammered, "I—I guess so."

Betsy led the way into the huge paneled kitchen, explaining that her mother stayed in her room when Betsy gave her Sunday evening parties and that her father had conveniently accepted an invitation to a lecture.

"Aren't my parents wonderful?" Betsy asked. "They're here when I need them, and they disappear when I have parties."

As she chatted on, telling Fran that she was glad she had managed to join the crowd that evening, Betsy lined up tall glasses on three small serving trays. She opened ice trays and stuffed chunks of ice into the glasses.

"Now," she said to Fran, "if you'll open the ginger ale and fill the glasses half-way, I'll add the punch. I didn't have time to mix this earlier, but one giant stir should make it taste just as good."

Betsy left soon with a tray of punch while Fran continued to pour the concoction into other glasses. Just as she reached the third tray, Joe walked in.

"Need any help?" he asked with an air of nonchalance.

Fran took a deep breath. "Did Betsy send you in for another tray?"

"I volunteered," he replied candidly. "I wanted a chance to talk to you."

Flustered at his presence now, Fran told him, "I've been out there all evening, and you've hardly spoken to me."

"Great day! I wouldn't dream of making your boyfriend jealous." Joe chuckled impishly. "He might be vicious."

Fran wasn't sure which annoyed her most, Joe's words or his infuriating manner. Coolly, she said, "Chris isn't the jealous type. Besides, we're not going steady, if that's what you're implying."

Joe straddled one of the kitchen stools, lifted a small stack of sandwiches from a tray, and began to munch on them. In between bites, he pointed out, "You might as well be going steady. He's the only boy I've seen you with in ages. Of course, I don't see you quite as often these days—"

"I could ditto that for you and Betsy!"

Joe drank some punch. "At least we stay in a crowd. But this guy keeps you all to himself—or is it vice versa?"

Fran set down the pitcher of punch and met Joe's dark eyes defiantly. "What are you trying to prove? You invited us here tonight. Remember?"

Joe waved a hand as if to ward off her verbal attack. "Don't get huffy about it! You know, all these weeks you've been buried in that studio, missing all sorts of parties —even that play. Then when you *do* go out, it's always with him. You could have a ball, Fran, if you mixed with a crowd."

"Thanks for the advice!" she managed flippantly. "I didn't know you cared!"

"You see how sensitive you are? You twist every remark into an insult."

"That's because they usually are!" Her hands were trembling so that she was certain she would drop the heavy pitcher if she tried to lift it. There was a stretch of silence, during which Joe didn't speak and Fran didn't even look up. Then, still wordlessly, Joe got up and left the room.

Fran sat down on one of the kitchen stools and tried to control her fury. I must hate him, she thought. I couldn't possibly like any boy as obnoxious as Joe Collier!

She moved woodenly through the rest of the evening, avoiding a glance in Joe's direction. Finally, on the way home with Chris, she relaxed a little. She even laughed at his gentle humor. Of course, Joe was right, Fran told herself. She and Chris were loners, and tonight she had discovered why. They were different from Joe and Millie's crowd because they spent their spare time working, while the others splurged on social activities.

Fran supposed now that it was this difference in their outlook, their reactions, that annoyed her and bothered them. One thing she was certain of: if she felt as miserable at future parties as she had tonight at Betsy's, she would cross them off her schedule forever.

10

The Linden-Carter Wedding

"Boy, that's the biggest ol' turkey we've ever had!" Jamie exclaimed. His blue eyes were reveling in the golden-brown expanse of a turkey that lay, breast upward, on the Avery dinner table.

"Fifteen pounds!" Mrs. Avery declared. "We'll be eating it for days." She removed her apron, smoothed her house dress, tugged at wayward wisps of hair, and then seated herself at the head of the table.

After grace was said, Linda spoke up. "I'm glad it's a big turkey because I mostly like the hash."

"I like this sweet-potato soufflé the best," Diane commented as she scooped a spoonful from the casserole topped with toasted marshmallows.

"The cornbread dressing was your father's favorite," Mrs. Avery told her family in a quiet voice, "and mine, too, I suppose." She held the pan for Fran, urging her to take a generous helping. "You've rushed around here so this week, you've scarcely had a full meal."

Fran served herself a small mound of the crusty dressing so richly seasoned with onions and celery. "Don't worry, Mother, I intend to stuff myself and then take a nap after the dishes are finished. I'll catch up on my chores tomorrow."

"The awful part about today," Diane interrupted, "is that it's Thursday—and no ballet lesson. I can hardly wait to show Mrs. King how well I can plié. Please notice that I said 'well' and not 'good.' She teaches me grammar, too, sometimes."

Mrs. Avery's laugh was gay. "I'm glad someone can get through to you, honey. Remind me to do something nice for Mrs. King."

"You could make her something for Christmas," Linda suggested. "We're already making aprons and pot holders at school."

"Please, Linda!" Fran's mother burst out. "Let's not discuss Christmas today. This is the nicest Thanksgiving dinner we've had in years. One thing at a time!"

Instinctively, Fran glanced at the girls and Jamie, who were staring at their mother with bewildered expressions. "It's really a wonderful dinner, Mother," Fran remarked, hoping to smooth the unpleasantness. "In fact, it's the best meal I've ever had. And we won't have to cook for days!"

Fran's mother smiled now. "That's part of the game, dear. Slave one and rest three. But there won't be much rest at the store this weekend—Thanksgiving sale." She laid her fork down and looked around at the little faces. She turned to Fran. "I want to thank you for handing me the money for all this food. I enjoy roasting a turkey so much that I took your money without a qualm—"

"But that's one of the reasons I'm working, Mother! If you feel up to it at Christmas, we'll have another turkey!"

Her mother patted her arm. "A nice ham might be better, but we'll wait and see."

With the atmosphere serene and the children eating heartily, Fran spoke up. "Mother, I do think we should discuss what we'd all like to get this year." With a glimpse at Jamie, she added, "So we can write our letters to Santa."

"Well, I want a piano!" Linda announced in a tone so fervent that everyone turned her way. "I don't need a new one—just a piano with all the keys covered that doesn't sound hoarse."

"Linda," Diane countered, "who do you think you are? You know Fran and Mother can't—I—I mean, you know Santa can't get a piano down our chimney!"

Jamie gave a gusty sigh. "Mama, don't they know there's no such thing as Santa Claus? Two summers ago Butch Hankins told *me*, and the whole third grade knows there isn't, so how come *they* don't know it?"

The others laughed uproariously. After they had calmed down, Mrs. Avery turned to Diane. "And what, my dear, do you want? A white wool skirt?"

Still giggling, Diane shook her pony tail. "No, I want some black leotards just like Mrs. King wears."

"All right, Jamie," Mrs. Avery said, "it's your turn."

With twinkling eyes, the child listed half the items on display in Draper's toy department. Then, at the children's insistence, Fran mentioned a few trinkets she would like to receive.

Just then the telephone rang, and Jamie scrambled to

answer. He returned, exclaiming, "Fran, it's for you! It's one of those Princes!"

"Mr. Prince?" Fran met her mother's glance. "What could he want today?"

Anxiously, Fran hurried out to the hall and picked up the receiver. "Hi, Fran, this is Greg. Hope I didn't disturb your meal, but I wanted to call early so you could make plans. Want to go along on a wedding assignment tonight? It's that Linden-Carter affair. Dad and I were supposed to do it, but he's pretty bushed. And he put away enough turkey to sink a submarine. Barbara's willing to give up a party to go, so this would be an ideal time for you to be initiated. The wedding's at eight, followed by a reception at the country club, but we'll have to get you at about seven to allow plenty of time for pictures before the wedding."

Fran gulped. She had looked forward to a quiet evening, but she longed to go with Greg on one of these assignments. After a mental survey of her closet, she exclaimed, "I'd love to go, Greg. May I wear a suit?"

"Sure. Barbara's wearing a black one so I can spot her among the pastel wedding finery."

The wedding guests, Fran thought, as she hung up the receiver. Shimmery satin and lace dresses brightened with dazzling jewelry. She shivered in excitement. Would they serve caviar with the punch and *petit fours*?

"Mother!" Fran rushed back to the kitchen, explaining the telephone call in snatches of joyous words. Finally, she assured her that Barbara, Greg's fiancée, had agreed to Fran's accompanying them.

Her mother's face didn't glow as Fran had expected, though. "You'll be paid for it, won't you?"

"Paid? I haven't thought of it. Mother, don't you understand? They're doing me a favor!"

Mrs. Avery put some dishes in the sink and began to run water over them. "I can't blame you for being thrilled, dear, but you've worked so hard today and you'll probably be out late."

"But with the studio closed tomorrow, I'll have time to sleep late and still get everything done. Haven't you noticed how well I've been organizing my time lately? I'll soon be as efficient as you."

"That, my dear, wouldn't be hard!"

Greg buzzed the doorbell promptly at seven, and Fran ushered him in and proudly introduced him to her family. With equal pride, she introduced her family to Greg, who stood hatless and snug in a trench coat, just inside the living room.

After a moment of polite conversation, Greg told Fran, "We'd better go, Fran. Barbara's waiting in the car, and it's a long drive."

Barbara Lane, Fran discovered, was even lovelier than her photo, which Greg kept on a wall in the darkroom. Auburn-haired, with flashing dark eyes and creamy skin, she was as chic as a Parisian model in her black suit and fur coat.

"I've been so anxious to meet you," she declared as Fran settled in the front seat beside her. "I have such tremendous admiration for you. Greg's amazed at how quickly you've caught on to the work. I do hope I won't make any blunders this evening!"

"Anyone as pretty as you, sweet," Greg teased, "would be forgiven immediately!"

Barbara laughed merrily. "Doesn't he say the nicest things? But we girls know that tonight the bride will be the center of all the attention."

"Well, I hope I can do justice to her," Greg said solemnly. "She's not only a plain girl, but she's the most unphotogenic I've encountered."

"Oh, no, Greg," Barbara responded sympathetically, "how awful!"

"It's just one of those things," Greg went on. "Helen Linden has a wonderful personality, but it doesn't come across in her photographs. I'll have to take a hundred, I guess, to make sure I get a few dozen good ones."

"Helen Linden," Barbara said quietly. "Didn't her family come into some money and then work their way into society? I remember a newspaper spread about her debut a few years ago."

"Dad and I did those pictures," Greg explained. "My parents knew the Lindens years before one of Mr. Linden's inventions was put on the market. Dad had always done their pictures, and they kept calling him in instead of some fancy society photographer. Helen insisted that I take her wedding pictures. I did her engagement photos and they were good and she knew it. But I worked hard with special lighting and later with a retouching brush to do her justice."

The Linden home was perched at the top of a long, sloping drive in the midst of a fashionable suburb. After Greg parked, the three crossed an immense flagstone terrace that was brightly illumined by floodlights. Fran glimpsed a swimming pool off to the right and a tennis court beyond it.

Greg stopped at a side door where a butler soon answered their ring. "Good evening, Jackson," Greg greeted him. "Good to see you again!"

"Good evening, ladies and Mr. Prince." The older man smiled. "Sure nice to have you here on this happy occasion!" He bowed slightly as he opened another door to a long hall. Leading the way, he took them through a maze of rooms and up the stairs to the second floor, where they quickly entered a luxurious bedroom.

Several women were fussing over a slender form clad in white satin and clouds of white tulle. When the girl recognized Greg, her angular features softened into a radiant smile. "Greg, you did make it! You know, I've just discovered why marriages are permanent. No one could bear this ordeal twice! Wouldn't you know," she rushed on excitedly, "the caterer was called out of town so we had to engage another. The bridal consultant was detained at another wedding, so she'll be late getting here, and Carl's father left his tails at home so he had to have someone bring them to him! Please, Greg," she mocked, "don't ruin the film!"

The young woman suddenly turned toward Barbara. "So *this* is your fiancée! I've been hoping I could meet the lucky girl. And who's this cute teen-ager?"

"Oh, I'm sorry," Greg broke in, quickly introducing Barbara and Fran to the bride-to-be. He added, "Fran's our new receptionist. I promised to bring her to a wedding sometime, so here she is."

Helen laughed softly. "Well, you couldn't have picked a better time to learn all the things that aren't supposed to happen!"

"Shame on you, child," an older woman scolded. "This will be a perfect wedding. All weddings have their moments, don't they, Greg?"

"Mrs. Linden!" Greg exclaimed. "I didn't recognize you there behind all that net."

"Dear, tactful Greg." The woman moved out from behind her daughter's billowy skirt. "My hair was a pale blue when you saw me last. A turquoise rinse is my favorite this year. Now, Helen, turn around once more. I think it's fixed."

Helen grimaced. "I tripped on one of the ruffles on my petticoat a while ago and tore it!"

Although she denounced her own efficiency, young Helen Linden calmly supervised a myriad of final details while posing for Greg's camera and continuing a stream of happy chatter.

Fran became entranced with the scene that unfolded before her. With Barbara holding the strobe light at certain angles, Greg took a number of photos from several positions with and then without the four women who were assisting Helen with her bridal finery. Helen insisted on having a few pictures taken with her mother while the latter hooked on her daughter's wedding pearls and then some with her maid-of-honor adjusting the bridal veil with its delicate circlet of pearls and orange blossoms. Mrs. Linden suggested one pose of her daughter accepting a borrowed handkerchief from the devoted cousin attending her and a blue satin garter from another, older cousin.

It became Fran's duty to unwrap the fresh film and to keep the used film separate from the unused. She learned much from listening to Greg's instructions to Barbara, and she began to understand the jargon of the photographer-on-assignment.

Then there were the pictures of Helen and her parents to be snapped as they climbed into the chauffeured limousine for the drive to the church. Hurrying ahead, Greg reached the church just before the Lindens arrived, and his camera was aimed at them when they alighted.

Having slipped through the side door, Helen and her entourage closeted themselves in the privacy of the church study, while Greg and Fran and Barbara went up the front steps. There they were greeted by an usher who let them enter without the necessary engraved invitation. A moment later, Fran paused at the entrance of the vast church auditorium. A forest of ferns and flowers, harmonizing with the pale gowns of the bridesmaids, formed the altar background. Above all this splendor was a magnificent cathedral ceiling. Soon the organist took her seat, and the church reverberated with the strains of a familiar concerto that signaled a flurry of activity, as bridesmaids and other attendants took their places in the vestibule.

"Well, girls," Greg said quietly, "get yourselves seats in the back row. I've got to take pictures in the vestibule as the wedding party goes by, but that will be all until the ceremony is over—except for some with natural light. The Lindens don't want the dignity shattered by a flashing strobe light."

He talked faster now. "But after the ceremony, I've got to take pictures of all the relatives and the bridal party—the groom's parents, the bride's parents, and so on. This feat has to be accomplished in about thirty minutes, before they all leave for the reception. So, girls, please help me corral them down at the altar and line them up. If that bridal consultant doesn't show up, I'll want you two to look out for sagging slips, tucked up hems, and all those things that men never notice until it's too late. One woman posed for Dad once with her shoes off!"

With a playful salute, Barbara replied, "Yes, sir! We'll be the most efficient assistants you've ever had!"

Fran sat rigidly throughout the ceremony. Now and then she glanced back to the spot where Greg was taking time exposures of the entire wedding scene, his 4x5 camera mounted on a tripod. These, Fran knew, required natural light, so that no flash or noise was involved.

The minister pronounced the couple man and wife, and they came back up the aisle, smiling right into the flash of

Greg's camera, which he had deftly unlatched from the tripod seconds before.

With Fran following directions, Barbara supervised the proceedings as if she had done it many times before. Beaming approval, Greg reached the front of the church and slid new film holders into his camera. Then he began to snap dozens of pictures, calling out various combinations of relatives and attendants. He changed film holders so rapidly that Fran marveled at his skill. Finally, Greg dismissed everyone except the bride and groom and the minister. He posed more pictures of the minister with the newlyweds, then the bride and groom together.

When the bride stood alone for her pictures, Greg came over to Fran. "Get some of that fast film out of my satchel, Fran. I'm going to try some natural light shots—they'll be a little softer. I'm trying my best to make this bride beautiful."

Just as they were leaving the church behind the new Mr. and Mrs. Carter, a number of wedding guests swarmed around, showering the couple with rice. While Barbara and Fran stood aside to enjoy the sight, Greg rushed over for a photo of the newlyweds surrounded by their well-wishers.

After the formality of the wedding, the reception seemed rather lively. Greg walked about taking candid pictures, capturing those precious moments when the young Carters were cutting their wedding cake, sharing first slices of it, and, later, sipping punch. There was another click just as the bride's bouquet was caught by a tiny flower girl. Finally, Greg managed to catch an outdoor shot of the couple settling into their new foreign car, just before it sped away into the darkness.

On the drive home, Barbara quietly teased Greg about their own wedding plans. "Will eight bridesmaids and three hundred wedding guests be enough, sir?"

Fran, leaning back against the seat, fastened her gaze on stars that blinked like rhinestones in a cold jet sky. She could hardly wait until she described this panorama to Millie. "Millie," she would declare, "it's enough to ban elopements forever!"

11

An Invitation

Fran awakened slowly to the sound of the furnace blower. It's strange, she thought, but I haven't been aware of that noise for weeks. Have I been that busy?

She could hear Linda and Diane giggling off in their bedroom, and Jamie— Where was he? She turned over and plowed her face under the pillow, thankful that Jamie was old enough to entertain himself in the early morning. She chuckled to herself as she remembered some of Jamie's mischievous moments. The morning he had arranged bacon strips in neat rows across the kitchen floor; the day he had dumped detergent powder down the furnace register; the hours he'd spent taking canned goods from the kitchen cabinets and putting the cans on the bookcases in the living room.

Suddenly, Fran's heart leaped. School! I'm late for school! Swiftly, she swung her legs around until she was sitting on the edge of the bed. It was then that she spied her brown suit hanging on the open door of the closet. It's Friday, she thought, relief surging through her, the day after Thanksgiving, the morning after the Linden-Carter wedding. It was a holiday! How had her mother left so quietly? And where *was* Jamie?

Fran slipped into her housecoat and went out to the kitchen. There she found the table cluttered with turkey slices lying half out of their wrapper of foil and surrounded by the peanut butter jar and the grape jam. A toaster and several knives and spoons added to the disorder.

"Jamie?" Fran called. Immediately, he came scampering into the kitchen, his mouth still circled with jam. "Jamie, how did you manage to make such a mess?"

"Oh, that." He shrugged. "I made a turkey sandwich. Peanut butter and jam on the bread and turkey in the middle."

Fran moaned. "For breakfast? Well, the next time you make a sandwich, please put the food back in the refrigerator so it won't spoil."

"OK, Sis. Can I turn on 'Space Squadron' now?"

"I guess so. The girls are awake, anyway."

Fran prepared some breakfast for herself and ate it leisurely, but her thoughts raced ahead, planning chores for the day. I'll call Millie first, she decided, and tell her about last night. When she dialed Millie's number, though, no one answered.

Fran went to her room and dressed, sorted out personal laundry, dunked lingerie in mild suds, and then tidied her room and polished shoes. She gave the girls their breakfast and supervised their chores.

After lunch was over and the kitchen clean, Fran set up the ironing board in the living room so that she could watch a movie on TV as she worked. She had tried Millie's number several times, but no one seemed to be home.

Chris called to inform her that he was going out of town with his parents to visit relatives over the weekend. "Imagine, my dad closing down today with Draper's packing in all those customers!"

"Well, after all, you aren't having a sale."

"Miss me a little, Fran?" Chris said then.

Surprised by the unexpected endearment, Fran's heart skipped a beat, but she kept her voice light as she teased, "I do already."

Diane soon confronted Fran with her immediate personal problem. After all the afternoons she'd been confined to the house to care for Linda and Jamie, she demanded, "I want to go to Peggy's for the rest of the afternoon!" Then Linda skipped away to play with little neighbors, too, and Jamie eventually fell asleep on the sofa.

Fran was marveling at the sudden quiet when the doorbell shrilled through her thoughts. Opening the door, she was startled to find Joe Collier there on the porch, huddled in his suburban jacket.

"Why, Joe! Won't—won't you come in?" She said it graciously, but she fully expected him to decline, certain that he'd dropped by only to give her a message or borrow something. Besides, their last encounter, she remembered now, had been anything but cordial.

Joe was smiling sheepishly. "Guess I should have called," he said, as he stepped inside, "but I—" He stopped, his eyes fastened on Jamie. "Sound asleep with that TV going!"

Fran gestured for Joe to sit down. Then she walked over and clicked off the TV.

As she went over to the iron, Joe spoke up. "Hey, don't let me ruin that schedule of yours!" His tone was light, without a trace of sarcasm. "My mother sometimes irons when neighbors drop in."

Fran had hesitated about ironing with Joe there, but after he used the word "neighbor," she went on with it. She didn't care if it was polite or not. If she was just a neighbor—someone Joe could treat as casually as he liked—she wasn't going to waste precious time and party manners on him.

Joe took his usual sprawling position in the easy chair and began to describe the chaos at the shopping center. "And Draper's—it's a madhouse! I mailed a special delivery for Dad and had to walk two blocks after I parked just to get to the post office. I wanted to go to Watts's, but it was closed—"

Fran said matter-of-factly, "Chris's family went out of town for the weekend."

Joe locked his hands behind his head. "Great day, but I feel like a loafer, kicking around home all day. Everyone else is going at top speed."

"Betsy, too?" Fran ventured. "I mean, she's probably made big plans."

"Yeah, she has. She's gone to a game at State U., and she's giving another party tomorrow night. More shrimp salad."

"I like shrimp salad," Fran declared, "especially the way it was served last night at Helen Linden's reception. They had caviar, too, and fancy little cakes, and just about everything."

"Helen Linden's wedding?" Joe brightened. "How did you rate an invitation to that blow-out?"

"I didn't. I went with Greg and his fiancée to help him take wedding pictures. It was just gorgeous. Eight bridesmaids and umpteen relatives! You never saw so much fur and jewelry."

Joe shook his head slowly. "What a ball! I'd like to have made the commission on all those rented tuxedos."

He was curious about other details, so Fran gave him an animated description of the evening. As she talked, she realized that Joe had listened intently without inserting even one derogatory remark. Then she was surprised when Joe launched into a full account of a society wedding he had once attended.

Presently, Fran asked, "Want something to drink, Joe? We have milk, punch, tomato juice, soft drinks—"

Right on cue, Jamie awakened. "Hey, Joe!" he exclaimed, rubbing his eyes. "You're here! Play me a game, Joe!"

It was an hour before Joe left. By then, the girls had returned, already urging Fran to prepare supper. They turned on the TV, promptly forgetting their guest as a circus program came into view.

Joe glanced at his watch. Picking up his jacket, he stood up. Fran moved toward him. "I'm sorry I've been so busy, Joe," she said, "but I'm glad you came." She hoped she sounded as sincere as she felt.

At the door, he turned, his dark eyes looking directly into hers. "Fran, I've been trying to get up nerve ever since Wednesday— Well, after the other night at Betsy's, I was afraid you'd slam the phone in my ear, but would you go to the Holiday Dance with me? That is, if you're not going with Chris."

Fran faltered. "The Holiday Dance—with you?" She shook her head, and her voice was hoarse as she told him, "I can't, Joe. The Princes have already warned me about how rushed we'll be that last week before Christmas. Chris isn't going either, for the same reason."

"But it's been changed, Fran! The dance was postponed until the twenty-seventh, a whole week later. I heard about it Wednesday afternoon. They're going to post the new date on the bulletin board on Monday—"

"The twenty-seventh?" Fran was overwhelmed by the change in the date. Only one small edge of her mind wondered why he was asking her, while all her instincts focused on one conviction—she couldn't refuse Joe's invitation. "I'd love to go with you, Joe!" she blurted out. "I'll rearrange my entire schedule just to be there," she promised.

"You won't change your mind at the last minute, will you?"

"Of course not!" she replied with a lightness that she hoped would match his. She wanted to tell him that it would be their first formal dance since a certain special evening in the tenth grade, but she really couldn't let him know that the occasion had been that special to her.

While her hands peeled potatoes, Fran's thoughts were joyful. It was incredible, unbelievable, impossible! Joe Collier had asked Fran Avery to the Holiday Dance!

As the children gathered for the evening meal, their chatter broke the spell. Now, Fran's ego began to smart. Had Joe already asked Betsy, and if so, why had she declined? Of course, she told herself, she didn't really care if she were Joe's tenth choice. At least he had asked her, and not at the last minute but a full month in advance.

When her mind reviewed Joe's visit, she felt annoyed once more at that word "neighbor." What's wrong with me? she wondered. Here Joe has asked me to the biggest dance of the year, and I'm miserable.

She tolerated the children and her chores that evening,

waiting for the moment when she had a chance to call Millie. Finally, when the children were in bed and her mother was in the living room, Fran went into the hall and dialed the McArdle number.

"Hello?" It was Millie's voice.

"Millie, I've tried to get you all day. I'm bursting with news!"

"Mother and I spent the day in town at the sales," she explained. "Fran, did you get a raise?"

"Better than that, Millie. I went to Helen Linden's wedding Thursday, but that can wait. . . . Millie," Fran exclaimed, "Joe asked me to go to the Holiday Dance with him!"

"Oh, *Fran*! You know, goose bumps are popping out all over me. Hey, you didn't pull that poor-working-girl routine at a crucial time like this?"

"I almost did, Millie, but now I won't have to—"

"Wow," Millie broke in, "would I love to see Betsy's face when she hears that Joe won't be twiddling his thumbs just because—" She stopped, and her voice softened. "Fran, honey, I'm sorry!"

Fran's voice shook a little. "That's all right, Millie. I was sure that Joe hadn't asked me first."

"But you don't understand," Millie rushed on, "Betsy *can't* go. She's leaving for New York on the nineteenth, the afternoon we get out for the holidays. They won't be back until the day after Christmas."

"Then Joe knew she'd be back on the twenty-seventh!" Fran exclaimed.

"And what," Millie inquired, "is happening on the twenty-seventh—another party?"

"That's the dance, Millie! They've postponed it a week. Joe found it out on Wednesday afternoon! Don't you see, Millie?" Fran went on, "Betsy could have gone with Joe and he knew it, but he asked me instead! Oh, Millie, I'm afraid I'll wake up and find it's just a dream."

"Fran, I've been telling you all along. Joe likes you best. He just hasn't found it out yet."

Fran's heart battled with her conscience all during the weekend. Monday, when the notice of the postponement of the dance was tacked on the bulletin board, moans were heard, although most students, Fran noted, were grateful for the change because the dance no longer conflicted with other parties and holiday plans.

Fran dreaded seeing Chris. She was afraid that he would want her to go to the dance with him. She left school early, still worrying over what she would say. Somehow she would have to convince Chris, without hurting him, that he wasn't—and shouldn't be—the only boy in her life.

She'd gone about a block beyond the school grounds when Chris's car drew up beside her at the curb. Fran greeted him gaily but guardedly as she climbed into the front seat and held her books tightly in her lap. Their conversation skipped immediately from the Watts's weekend trip to the forthcoming dance.

"Talk about a break for us," Chris began. "How about it, Fran? Want to go?"

Fran stared out at the street, carefully avoiding his eyes. "Chris, I am going—with Joe Collier. He asked me last week."

"Oh," Chris said. "Well, he must have had some inside information because they just— Or did you change your mind and decide to 'burn the candle at both ends' that week?" He chuckled, "Or is that 'burn the midnight oil'? I'm not too good on those adages."

"No, Chris," Fran rushed on soberly, "I didn't change

my mind about the dance until Joe told me about the change. He just happened to be there when the meeting ended—when they decided to delay the dance. But, Chris, there's more to it than that." She struggled to keep her voice casual. "Chris, don't you think we've been seeing each other too much? I mean, so exclusively. We really should date other people, because everyone's beginning to pair us off as steadies."

"And that," Chris broke in, "is what you want to avoid?"

"Well, after all, you haven't really given yourself a chance to get acquainted with any other girls."

He gave her a long, searching look, then a smile spread across his face. "All right, I'm convinced. We'll be that disgusting cliché—just good friends."

12

A Crisis at the Studio

As Fran lifted the receiver from the buzzing telephone, her eyes instinctively reviewed the assortment of customers. Every sofa in the reception room was jammed, and two benches that Greg had brought in earlier from the utility room were crowded.

"Prince's Photos," Fran spoke into the receiver.

"Hi, slave! This is Millie, hoping you can lunch with me. I'm finishing up my Christmas shopping today. You're not the only efficient one, you know."

Fran sighed tiredly. "Don't be funny, Millie. I haven't bought a thing. I just made my list last night."

"Why, Fran, this is the first Saturday in December. There are only two more after this before Christmas!"

"Look, Millie, I haven't time to worry about the other two Saturdays. I'm having enough trouble with this one. The studio is packed! Come by and I'll see if I can get away."

"You're discouraging me, Fran. I was planning to surprise my parents with a photo. One that *I* paid for," she added playfully, "but I think I'll wait until next spring and just give them graduation pictures."

"Oh, dear! As a conscientious employee, Millie, I should insist that you need pictures for both occasions!"

"Of course," Millie mocked, "but the question is, can I afford them?"

"Well, we're running a special up to the fifteenth. If you buy one 8 × 10 portrait and twelve of the wallet size, you can get all thirteen pictures for less than the regular price. This is a fixed special—the amount and the price. As Greg explained it, this way the studio makes a better profit on the time involved. So many customers ask for wallet sizes at Christmas that the studio loses money unless they sell other photos along with them, because the wallet sizes require so much darkroom time. Anyway, it's really a popular offer. We're selling scads of them."

"Hmmm," Millie replied. "Maybe I'd better be different and not take the offer." After a moment, though, Millie consented and agreed to an appointment for the following Thursday. "Aren't you glad all your customers aren't as wishy-washy as I am?"

"It's elementary," Fran teased. "Yes!"

When the call ended, Fran wrote Millie's name down beside a cancellation for four-thirty on Thursday afternoon. That, she reflected, should be a happy occasion.

Shortly before lunch, Mr. Prince came out into the reception room. Fran noticed immediately that his gait was slower and his broad grin had shrunk to a feeble smile. She slid off the counter stool so that her employer could sit down. "Mr. Prince," she whispered anxiously, "is anything wrong?"

The man rubbed a hand across his ruddy face. In a weary voice, he asked, "How many appointments are scheduled for the afternoon, Fran?"

She scanned the appointment book. "From one until six o'clock there are ten," she replied, "but some of them are family groups. Mr. Prince," she added, "you look so tired. Is there anything I can do?"

"Yes, child. Call me a cab. I think I'll go home for awhile, but I don't feel like driving and Greg will need the car anyhow. He's too busy to take me. I hope it won't burden him to put off his darkroom work until tonight. He's taking over at the camera for me now—"

He looked around the room and then whispered to Fran, "If you get too rushed out here, just tell the customers to come back next week. If my wife's mother wasn't with us, Mrs. Prince could pitch in. But Greg called Barbara, and she's coming over after she leaves the hair dresser." Mr. Prince heaved a sigh that only sharpened Fran's concern.

"Don't worry about us," she told him gently. "You just rest today, and you'll be good as new." She called the local cab company then. She had dialed the number so often for customers that she knew it well.

After she had hung up, one of the customers sitting nearby stepped up to the counter. "Mr. Prince," she whispered, "I couldn't help overhearing. I'll be glad to drive you home. My car's in the parking lot at the back."

Mr. Prince beamed and shook his head. "Thank you, Mrs. Peterson, but Mac's held that cab company together with nothing but courage for three years now. I like to call on him every chance I get."

Mrs. Peterson smiled understandingly. "Well, just take care of yourself so you can enjoy a nice Christmas."

Fran went over to the coat rack and lifted off Mr. Prince's heavy overcoat. Returning to the counter, she held it while he slipped his arms into the sleeves. "Mac said he'd send a cab down immediately," Fran told him, "and he keeps his word." Her fingers began fumbling with the buttons on his overcoat.

Mr. Prince chuckled as he looked down at her. "Is this one of the services our customers get these days?"

"Oh, dear!" Fran gasped as she jerked her hands away. "It's just habit, I guess," she added, her face growing warm. "I've buttoned on coats for so many winters, I—"

He patted her arm affectionately. "Never mind, Fran. I was enjoying the special attention!"

Concerned only with her employer now, Fran deserted the counter long enough to walk Mr. Prince to the curb and wait until the cab arrived. She returned just in time to catch the ringing of the telephone.

Soon, a group of customers filed out of the portrait room with Greg following. Leaning over the counter toward Fran, he inquired about his father. After Fran had related the details, Greg said, "He wouldn't let me take him home, and he wouldn't consider canceling today's appointments. I don't mind taking over, but sometimes I wish he'd worry more about himself and less about the customers."

He picked up the appointment calendar and studied it. "Well, Fran, we've got a busy afternoon ahead, but we can still live it up. Call up Pete's Palace and order two of those steak sandwiches with all the trimmings, and don't worry about making the customers hungry. They can go out and eat."

Greg turned then and called out the twelve-thirty appointment. "Mrs. Higgins?"

A tall, slender young girl, not much older than Fran, came forward. "My husband's just gone into the Army," she explained as she walked away with Greg. "I want to send him a picture for Christmas."

The glass door opened again and Millie, bundled in her tomato-red coat, rushed over, dumping several sacks down on the counter in front of Fran. Rubbing her white gloved hands together, Millie exclaimed, "Fran, it's freezing out there!"

When she finally mentioned lunch, Fran explained her predicament. "I'm sorry, Millie, that I can't go out with you, but I'll be glad to share my snack with you. Greg and I have steak sandwiches ordered from that new place, Pete's Palace."

Millie shrugged. "I'll grab something at the grill, honey. Besides, I'm meeting Pete for a soda later, so I could wait." Her gaze flitted around the crowded room. "I don't blame poor Mr. Prince for going home. I wouldn't blame you, either. I'd quit if I had to face all this!"

"Millie," Fran chided, "it isn't as rushed as it looks. It's really fun meeting all these people. Of course, it gets hectic sometimes when the telephone rings."

At that instant, as if on cue, the telephone rang. Fran and Millie burst into laughter, and one of the customers near them smiled broadly.

"Prince's Photos," Fran began in the tone Diane now called her "studio" voice, "Miss Avery speaking."

"Miss Avery," a woman replied curtly, "could I have some pictures made today, or do I have to have an appointment?"

"Yes, you do. I mean, you must have an appointment. But we're booked up for today. We have several openings next week, though, and two openings for next Saturday—"

"My horrors, I can't wait that long! I wanted one made today while my permanent wave is still new."

"I'm awfully sorry," Fran replied sympathetically, "but we're booked almost solid for Christmas photos."

"Well, I'll just have to get another photographer, then!" The woman slammed the receiver down in Fran's ear. Flinching from the bang, Fran replaced the receiver on her end.

"Some woman wanted us to take her picture today," Fran said to Millie, "or else! So—it was else. She didn't like it!"

Millie had her purchases spread out over the counter. Fran tried to listen and look as her friend discussed them, but there were constant interruptions.

Mrs. Higgins soon returned, so Fran sent in the next customer. Two young girls came in and ensconced themselves in the dressing room. Then a delivery boy arrived with a cardboard box full of steaming hot food.

"If that stuff tastes as good as it smells," Millie declared, "Pete's Palace has won itself a new customer!" She dumped her packages into a big shopping bag and, just as she was leaving, told Fran, "If you get around to buying anything, call me, and we can wrap gifts together tomorrow."

Next to Millie, Barbara was the most welcome sight of Fran's day. Swathed in fur, the young woman brushed compliments aside and apologized for being delayed. "I just had to go by and see about Greg's father," she confided to Fran. "Their physician had just left. It's nothing serious, thank goodness. He's just been overworking."

Barbara hung up her fur coat and joined Fran at the counter. With her auburn hair swirled in a fresh hair-do, her figure trim in a simple black sheath dress, Barbara was, Fran decided, the most attractive girl who had visited the studio all day.

"I'm so glad you're here," Fran admitted now. "Greg and I had lunch sent over, but I'd love to go out just for a breath of air, even cold air!"

"Be my guest, then!" Barbara laughed softly, reading over the appointments for the afternoon. "Take an hour, if you'd like, Fran. I think I can make it from here."

Fran wasted no time accepting Barbara's generosity. She bounded down the block, buttoning her coat along the way. An hour! Well, she'd already eaten, so she might as well shop. She turned into the neon-sparkle of a variety shop and headed for the toy counter. On the way, she paused at an exhibit of costume jewelry. A large woman was sitting behind a counter, engraving names on some silvery bracelets and lockets for customers queued up beside her machine.

Fran's curiosity soon changed to interest. As she examined the dainty lockets, she decided that she would have one inscribed for Diane and another one for Linda.

That evening after the children were asleep, Fran brought her treasures into the living room. Her mother sat there in an easy chair before the TV, her hands busy with a lapful of mending.

Fran opened the two slender boxes and dangled the lockets in front of her. "Aren't they pretty, Mother?" She handed them over for a closer inspection. "You know how the girls enjoy identical gifts—especially things with their names on them. They're nice for the money, don't you think?"

"I suppose so," Mrs. Avery agreed, "but I'm more concerned about your working conditions than the money you earn for such trinkets! Greg Prince called you this evening and told you that his father wouldn't be able to return to work until after Christmas, and you accepted it as if he'd said he'd take a day off. I don't understand, Fran. How can the studio operate without him?"

Fran returned the lockets to their boxes and closed the lids. "Mother, Greg can do anything his father can at the studio. He's been helping him since he was a young boy. He's cutting classes at Junior College, and he'd be out for the holidays next week, anyway. Greg will just take his father's place—"

Fran's mother was frowning. "Why don't they hire extra help for the holiday season?"

"Because," Fran said patiently, "it's almost impossible to find an experienced person who's available for temporary work. It's like any other kind of job, I guess. If a person is skilled enough to be hired at all, he's usually good enough to be employed full-time. But I've told you before, Mother, the rush is over after Christmas."

"Well, I never imagined so many people gave pictures at this time of year. I don't remember doing so except when you and the girls were babies."

"You see, Mother? Married couples give pictures of their children to their families. Sweethearts exchange pictures, and teen-agers swap them. And those are just the photos made at the studio. Greg has outside pictures—weddings and banquets and parties."

"But you're just a young girl, Fran. Greg can't expect you to help him with all that work!"

"Mother!" Fran was struggling to control her exasperation. "I won't be the only one helping. Barbara's willing to help—for nothing—so why can't I for time-and-a-half? Greg promised that if I have to work past my usual time, he'll pay me for it."

"That's entirely beside the point to me, Fran. As for Barbara, she's a mature young woman. I'm sure she hasn't as much to do at home as you."

Fran felt tears stinging her eyes. "Mother, please don't make me quit now. Greg needs me and I—we—need the money. Besides, I won't work any harder. I'll just let something else go temporarily."

Mr. Avery shook her head. "I don't know what else you can let go. You scarcely take the time to eat a full meal now."

Weary from the effort to convince her mother and too tired at the moment to care, Fran got up and planted a kiss firmly on her mother's cheek. "It's late, Mother, and it's time we were in bed."

Through the fog of sleep, Fran remembered something else that Greg had told her about the Holiday Dance. He had promised his father that he would be there as scheduled to take the photographs. It was unlikely that another competent photographer would accept such an assignment on short notice. Besides, Mr. Prince took great pride in knowing that he offered the students a quality picture at a price they could afford.

Fran had forgotten to mention to Greg that she was attending the dance. He'll be surprised, she thought sleepily. Everyone will be surprised to learn that I'm going with Joe.

13

Fran Accepts the Challenge

The special Yule photo offer, which brought customers flocking into the studio, was a cash-and-carry transaction. Because Greg had maintained a steady output and three-day service on the proofs, few of the customers needed to be notified. Greg and Barbara took over the chore of telephoning the rest to inform them that their final photo orders were completed.

Even so, Fran's afternoons were clogged with customers dropping by to pick up their proofs. She felt confused by all the names and details she had to remember. "Bring your proofs back as soon as possible," she said to each customer. "Mr. Prince is hoping to finish Christmas work by the twentieth."

Mrs. Peterson was one of those pushing toward the counter on Wednesday afternoon. Fran handed over the manila envelopes almost mechanically. When Mrs. Peterson accepted hers, she said graciously, "You people are so wonderful and so brave to keep this place going without Mr. Prince. Give him my best, will you?"

"I will," Fran promised, but the woman's words pricked at Fran's sense of justice. Long before this crisis, Fran had been aware that Greg worked as hard as his father, but there was a distinct difference in their approaches to their jobs. Mr. Prince accepted the studio as a cross he had to bear, while Greg regarded it as a challenge. Oh dear, she thought now, here I go parroting one of Mrs. Suder's sociology lectures!

Fran glanced at the wall clock. It was nearing six-thirty, and a dozen customers clamored around the counter. A freckle-faced boy stepped up next. "Name's Sellers. My mother said you had our proofs ready."

"What day were they made?" Fran asked.

"Gosh, I dunno. Last week sometime, I think."

"Sellers—Sellers," Fran repeated, turning toward the stack of proofs that she hadn't yet had time to arrange alphabetically.

After a moment of searching, she exclaimed, "Here they are!" Handing the photos over, she added, "Our price list is enclosed in the envelope, and the deposit is paid. Tell your mother to choose the best ones and bring them back as soon as possible."

As the boy sauntered out, Fran glimpsed Chris among the customers. His eyes were questioning her. Fran shook her head and gestured helplessly. Chris shrugged, then turned and disappeared into the dusk outside.

It was the third afternoon this week that Chris had stopped by, but, Fran reflected now, it was the first time he had looked peeved. But I can't help it, she thought defensively, this is my job.

"Girlie—" An older woman was rapping on the counter. "We're still here, waiting for service."

"Oh, I'm sorry!" Fran stammered, her cheeks flaming. "Look, there must be a quicker way to do this. Let me bring all the proofs over here to the counter, and I'll call the names out as I come to them."

She quickly scooped up the small envelopes and spread them on the counter top. "Brown," she called out, "six poses of baby."

"That's mine!" a young woman in the back yelled as she pushed her way to the front.

"The deposit's paid," Fran told her. "Higgins," she called out while Mrs. Brown was turning away.

"That's my sister," a young girl spoke up. "I'm getting them for her."

Encouraged by the success of the new procedure, Fran continued through the stack, laying aside the envelopes that brought no response. Within ten minutes, the reception room was cleared. She pulled down the white shades on the glass door, emptied ash trays, and tidied up the magazines, ready to close up.

Soon Greg appeared with a wry smile. "It was so quiet out here, I decided that you'd ordered everyone to leave. What happened?"

Fran chuckled. "I decided to bring Mohammed to the mountain—or something like that." She quickly described the change she had made in the customary routine.

Greg shook his head in amazement. "And it made that much difference? Well, we should have done that ages ago."

Driving her home, Greg reminded Fran to keep a record

of how late she worked every day. "We've got to keep this businesslike, you know."

Fran replied playfully, "Don't worry, I'll remind you. It was fifteen minutes tonight!"

He asked Fran then if she'd be willing to come to his house on Saturday night and help his family and Barbara get out the backlog of reorders on the Linden-Carter wedding. The ordinary stamping and preparing for mailing had to be done, of course, and in addition the negatives had to be labeled and studio records brought up to date before the job could be filed away.

"Saturday night?" Fran asked, groping to remember if she had planned anything. She told herself that it couldn't be too important because it had completely slipped her mind. "Yes, Greg," she said, "I'd be glad to help."

"Fine," Greg replied. "With all of us pitching in, we should get it over with in one evening. Fran, we certainly appreciate the way you've stood by us. I don't know how we'll ever be able to repay you—"

Fran gulped. She hadn't expected compliments. She felt that she didn't deserve them, because she had a sense of satisfaction in her work that more than compensated for the time and toil involved. Her family needed her; the entire Prince clan relied on her; and now most of Waverly Park depended on her efficiency with Christmas photos. All she could put into words was simply "I love my job, Greg."

Fran walked into the kitchen just as the children were finishing with dessert. While her mother had a second cup of coffee, Fran served herself. Soon, she was explaining her Saturday night plans, hardly aware of the spaghetti she was eating.

Instantly, Diane interrupted. "Glory, Fran, you've got a date with Chris, remember?"

Instinctively, Fran glanced at her mother. "I—I forgot. We made it so long ago. I'll call him now," she said, pushing away from the table.

"No, Fran," her mother protested, "you shouldn't break that date! You don't owe the Princes your personal life, too! Even if they paid double-time, it still wouldn't be worth it!"

"But, Mother, I can date Chris anytime. After Christmas, I'll have months and months of weekends to date him."

With an expression of helplessness, Fran's mother turned away and silently stirred her coffee. Fran wavered between guilt and dismay, but the prospect of an interesting evening at the Princes, working with all those beautiful photos, was like a tempting dessert frosted with delectable green dollars.

"I don't mind, Mother," Fran assured her, "and neither will Chris!"

Fran greeted Chris warmly when he answered the phone. "I'm sorry I wasn't ready to leave, Chris. So many people come by after they get off from work."

"I'm afraid I was rude," Chris said, "stalking out of there without a word. But when I saw that mob around you, I went blank. Boy! Can't you send some of that business down our way?"

"They were just picking up pictures," she told him. "Very dull. But thanks for stopping by for me again."

"Anything for a friend," he teased.

"Chris—" Fran began solemnly. "The reason I called you— Well, it's about our date Saturday night. I'll have to break it, Chris. I'm sorry, but Greg and his parents want me to come over and help them. You remember that big wedding I went to? Well, all the rich relatives want copies of the pictures. Even Barbara will be over there helping, so you can see it's urgent."

"If it's so important," Chris broke in, "how can it wait until Saturday night?"

"He's not through printing them yet—" Fran didn't finish because she suddenly realized Chris's words were drenched with sarcasm. "Look, it's an emergency, and it's part of my job. Couldn't we just postpone our date until the next Saturday?"

His voice was low. "I can't make it, then. Dad's already collared me to help him restock some shelves that night."

"You see?" Fran blurted. "It's part of every job." She laughed softly, then, hoping to erase his disappointment. "We might as well face it—we're two of a kind."

Chris soon assured her that he wasn't annoyed, but although the call ended pleasantly, Fran reviewed their conversation like a worrisome assignment. She was fond of Chris; she cherished his friendship.

The children began to claim so much of her attention that she eventually dismissed Chris from her thoughts. Linda insisted on playing her latest "piece," and in the living room, Diane donned her ballet shoes and performed the new steps she had learned.

"Fran," she said, "see how much prettier a plié is when I do it the way Mrs. King taught me?"

Jamie, lolling on the sofa, observed, "That's just a squat, Diane. Just a silly squat!"

"It's a plié!" Diane yelled. "That's a French word. See how graceful it is?" While Diane bent her knees outward and away from one another, one arm swept up and across her body, past her face, until it extended above her head.

"I'll have to take your word for it, Diane," Fran admitted wearily. "It looks OK to me, but then, you've always looked graceful."

"Glory!" The child stamped her foot now. "Can't you

tell? Mrs. King said my arms are better." She insisted on repeating the movement once more. "Then there's my new pirouette," she went on, as she spun about on one foot. "I'm supposed to let my arm push me, but it's so *hard!*"

Fran blinked in the direction of her sister, who was now a whirling blur. It's maddening, she thought. I'm so tired, and Diane is bursting with energy.

She finally escaped by declaring that she had a mountain of homework. Settling on her bed in her room and opening her Lit 3 notebook, she fretted over the book report that had nagged at her for days. She had completed three pages so far.

After reading it over again, she decided that it sounded all right. It wasn't her best one, and there was a word she wasn't certain about. She knew that Mr. DeLong was a stickler for correctly spelled and properly used words, but the dictionary was in the living room. It's too far away, she told herself miserably. When she considered the alternative, she still didn't care. What would be so earth-shaking about one small misspelled word?

Riding to school with Joe the next morning, Millie reminded Fran that this was the afternoon for her appointment at the studio. "I brought two blouses, Fran, so I could choose. Should I wear earrings?" She held a pair of pearl ones against her ears.

"It's up to you, Millie," Fran replied. "Some do, some don't."

"Well, listen to Miss Enthusiastic! Maybe I should cancel that appointment. My hair doesn't look too good anyway."

Fran hunched further down in her heavy coat. "I'm sorry I was curt, Millie," she said quietly. "I feel as if I'd spent the night at the laundromat, tumbling around in a dryer."

"Oh, Fran!" Millie was gentle now. "You shouldn't study so late every night!"

"I didn't study as much as usual last night. After that mad pace at the studio, I didn't feel like studying. And yesterday I cut art class so I'd have time for Christmas shopping. If you two don't see much of me in the next week or two, just look for me at the studio, buried under Christmas pictures!"

"How's Mr. Prince doing, Fran?" Joe inquired.

"Just fine. He calls up almost every day to check on things."

After they reached the school, Millie hurried away to meet Pete Cassidy for their early morning chat. Joe walked with Fran to her homeroom. "I'll be down at the shopping center this afternoon," he told her, "so I could give you a lift home. Unless Chris has taken it on as a regular job."

Fran glanced at him in surprise. She'd almost convinced herself that the Holiday Dance was a fluke, that Joe had asked her purposely to prove to Betsy that she really wasn't the only girl in his life. But now—

"Chris has such a stiff schedule that he likes to get home before I even get off from work," Fran confessed. "He's been wonderful about stopping by for me when he could, but I'm usually tied up with customers and he can't wait. I try to leave about six-thirty—"

"Then I'll come in and wait." With a casual flip of the hand, he was gone.

That afternoon, when Chris drove her down to the studio as he had done often lately, she told him that Joe would be taking her home. "Good," he said, with no further comment.

:

True to his word, Joe sauntered into the studio shortly before six-thirty, settled himself on one of the brown sofas, and watched the customers come and go. When the reception room was finally emptied, Fran began stamping proofs and slipping them into envelopes and attaching name and address labels. Joe came over promptly and picked up the rubber stamp bearing the name, address, and phone number of the studio.

"Here," he said, "I'll stamp while you stuff." He pulled the collection of maroon proofs closer and carefully applied the rubber stamp on the back of each one, admiring his handiwork now and then. When Greg appeared, Fran introduced the two. Smiling, Greg asked, "You wouldn't be interested in an after-school job, would you?"

Joe quickly shook his head. "No, *sir*! I'm tied up with basketball practice now. This is my afternoon off from that."

Greg placed a group of finished photos on the counter. "We can leave these, Fran. Barbara can do them in the morning. Do you have a ride home?"

"Yes, Greg. Joe's driving me. Thanks."

Traffic was heavy all the way down to the corner of Maple Avenue and Dozier Drive, where Joe turned left. He had monopolized the conversation with basketball, and then he began to discuss a party to be given by a friend of Betsy's. Fran had scarcely listened, for she was already involved in the chores awaiting her at home. The word "Saturday" finally penetrated her thoughts.

"Fran," Joe repeated, "I asked you if you and Chris could go Saturday night?"

Vaguely, she remembered that Saturday was filled. "No," she blurted, "I couldn't."

"But it won't begin until eight-thirty!" He sounded annoyed as he went on, "You're not the only girl with a job, Fran. There are plenty at school who work on Saturdays in Draper's and other stores. Somehow, they manage to get to parties."

By then she was too provoked to explain the truth to Joe concerning Saturday night. Instead, she flared, "It sounds so simple to you! Two whole hours between my job and a party. But after I eat supper, I have to do umpteen things that other girls who work on Saturdays don't have to do. If my mother wasn't working, my job would really be a lark. She could keep up my clothes, manage the kids alone, and have a hot supper all ready and waiting for me—!"

"Great day, don't bite me!" He turned into her driveway then and flicked off the ignition. "Fran, you're only kidding yourself. You manage to have plenty of time when Chris snaps his fingers, but for the rest of us—all your old friends—you're too busy. That job's making a snob of you."

"A *snob*!" Fran felt words rushing to her tongue, but the shock of his comment choked them off. She turned to get out of the car, and Joe scrambled out and came around to open the door for her.

"Fran," he said huskily, "I'm sorry. I didn't mean to hurt you. I was just thinking of you— After all, that's just supposed to be a part-time job you have, not a life sentence."

"I know," Fran said, trying to smile. "Now, if I tell you the real reason I can't go to that party, you'll say I'm their personal slave." She explained tersely, even including the fact that she'd broken a date with Chris.

Joe didn't say any more. He turned, his face stoic, and walked back to his car. Fran went into the house, telling herself that this was Joe, the boy who'd asked her to the Holiday Dance, the one she'd scrapped with since the summer they were six. She couldn't let any of this make any difference—now.

After supper, Fran stole a few moments of peace in the living room. Lying supine on the sofa, she covered her face with a pillow and closed her eyes. Maybe I am doing too much for the Princes, she thought. Maybe they've taken advantage of me, and I've been too naive to realize it. Still, she felt grateful to them and flattered that they'd given her, an inexperienced high school girl, such a responsible position.

Well, she told herself, no matter how hard the Princes expected her to work, she wouldn't give up her job. She'd gone too far now to turn back.

14

The Day Fran Will Never Forget

"Wouldn't you know?" Millie remarked, above the clatter of the cafeteria. "The first day we've managed to have lunch together in ages, and we can't even find seats."

"I just couldn't get here a minute sooner," Fran replied, as she followed her friend, who was balancing a lunch tray holding two cartons of milk and two slices of coconut pie.

"Hey!" Millie came to a sudden halt. "There are two empty stools and some knee-rubbing space at the end of that table beside the radiator. OK?"

Fran nodded wearily. "I'm in no position to argue. They seem to be the only empty stools."

While Millie unloaded the tray, Fran stacked their books

on the floor. Then she sat down and tore into her lunch sack.

"You must have flunked a test, Fran. You look so glum. Let's see— You just had Lit 3. It's elementary then—Mr. DeLong didn't like your theme."

"Book report," Fran corrected her. "Let me read you his fascinating comment." Opening her notebook, she jerked out the folded pages she'd received only minutes before. She read: " 'This sounds as if you had copied it from a book jacket. It lacks originality, and you're careless about details. Judging this by your usual standard, I can't give you more than a C-plus.' "

Millie gasped. "Fran, you've never made less than a B on a book report, have you?"

"No, but he's right. It isn't up to my usual standard, and I knew it when I handed it in."

She bit into her ham sandwich, telling herself that it was delicious even though she had forgotten to add mayonnaise. It only reminded her of the early morning scene with the children. Jamie had knocked over his cup of cocoa, and Diane had fumed because Fran had forgotten to press a certain skirt for her. Linda, who usually accepted the morning rush with placid patience, burst into tears when Fran informed her that she couldn't play at a friend's house that afternoon as she had planned to do.

"Mother insisted that you all stay here until one of us comes home," Fran had explained to the children. "She's going by the grocer's after work, and I'll be later than usual. I have an errand to do before I come home."

When the three persisted in prying, she snapped at them. "It's a secret, so stop picking at me!"

Fran forced herself to swallow. How could I have lost my temper so easily? she wondered. It was only natural for them to be curious.

"Fran," Millie spoke then, "what's *wrong*?"

Fran shook her head. "Just about everything. I fussed at the kids this morning, and I lost a world history assignment so the teacher gave me an F. I can make it up by doing it over, of course, but even if I make an A, it will still average a C—"

"Oh, Fran, you're just spreading yourself too thin! The Christmas rush is on and all, but there's only so much one person can do!"

"Well," Fran said thoughtfully, "I suppose I'd rather be rushed than suffer from a guilty conscience, and that's what I'd have if I deserted the Princes when they needed me most. Besides, it's worth all the work to see the girls so happy with their lessons, Millie. They've really been cooperative since they've been taking dancing and music. It makes them feel so—special."

After a pause, Millie conceded, "You're probably right, Fran. You usually are. But I've never been able to figure out why the ones who have the most responsibilities are always the ones who shoulder other people's problems. And while I'm being so nosey, mind if I ask what you and Joe were cooking up this morning on the way to school?"

"Oh, that!" Fran brightened. "Joe's driving me out to Martin's wholesale house this evening to buy Jamie a bicycle for Christmas. The other day I mentioned the sale, and Joe offered to take me out there, bring the bike back in his car, and hide it in his basement until Christmas Eve. There won't be any more Friday basketball games until after the holidays, so he has time to spare."

Millie's gray eyes twinkled. "Hmmm, wonder what this will do to Betsy's plans? She's invited half the school over tonight to celebrate Waverly High holding first place in district basketball. You know Betsy—any excuse for a party!"

"He'll be home in plenty of time, Millie," Fran assured her. "I made certain of that before I'd agree."

"Well," Millie teased, "at least you'll have him for an hour or so before that new perfume that Betsy's been gagging everyone with devastates him. Wonder where she got that stuff?"

Fran laughed then, a genuine laugh. "Millie, can't you just picture all the hand-holding going on while Joe shifts from first to second all the way out Kensington Boulevard in the Friday-evening traffic?"

Millie's voice was low, confidential. "Seriously, Fran, what's the score between you and Joe these days? He's taking you to the big dance, but he takes Betsy everywhere else!"

Fran dug her fork into the fluffy coconut pie. "Your guess is as good as mine, Millie. My pet theory is that I'm the handy old friend and neighbor he's using to remind Betsy that she doesn't really own him."

"That's elementary, Fran. Most of us pull that trick now and then. That's how I keep Pete on his toes. But, you know, Joe could impress Betsy a lot easier by walking you to classes every day, or something like that. The Holiday Dance, though, is serious. I can't imagine Betsy taking that gracefully."

To Fran's relief, the fifth-period bell rang. On the way to sociology, Fran wished there were some way she could escape that class today. Since the semester had begun, she had found it difficult to concentrate on Mrs. Suder's lengthy lectures. A joke around school was that as a baby Mrs. Suder had been fed stewed encyclopedias instead of oatmeal. On and on she would talk, first from the textbook, then from that vast library she had consumed during her forty years.

Fran considered Mrs. Suder a pleasantly attractive teacher.

She wore tailored clothes and had clipped hair that framed her face with dark, wispy curls. Even so, she seemed more like a robot than a warm human being.

Fran was barely settled at her desk when she began to feel drowsy. It was stuffy, and the room was so over-heated that it became sheer torture to keep her eyes open. Fortunately, she sat behind Anna Marie Hartwell, who had the broadest back in the entire class, so she felt well hidden from Mrs. Suder's view.

After the day's assignments were out of the way, the teacher suggested a class discussion. Several students began to participate, but Mrs. Suder inserted short lectures be-tween each person's remarks. After a while, Fran laid her head down on top of her books. Just for a minute, she told herself. It was so comfortable that she had no desire to move. How wonderful it would be, she thought, to close her eyes. She seemed to be floating in a black void with voices throbbing back and forth. Then, suddenly, she felt hands on her shoulders, shaking her.

"Fran Avery, wake up this instant!"

Fran shuddered, and her eyes flew open. When she no-ticed the circle of grinning faces, she sat up.

". . . falling asleep in my class!" Mrs. Suder was saying in a tone of disgust. "The bell has rung, Fran. Report to me after school!"

"Yes, ma'am," Fran choked out as she gathered her books. While her face burned, she shut her ears to the snickering that followed her up the corridor. How, she wondered miserably, could I have done such a thing? She was grateful that art was her last class. It was restful to whittle on the linoleum block that she planned to use to print her own Christmas cards, and it gave her time to re-gain her composure.

When Fran reached her locker after the sixth-period

bell, Millie was waiting for her. "Fran," she fumed, "of all the classes to pick for a nap! I survived Mrs. Suder's sociology lectures last year, you know. She thinks every word she utters is precious!"

Fran stared at her friend. "How did you find out?"

"Why, it's all over the school! Well, almost," she corrected herself. "Betsy's crowd is making bets on what punishment Mrs. Suder will give you. Don't worry, Fran, I'm going with you. I intend to tell the Great Stone Face exactly why you fell asleep!"

"Millie, don't you dare! I'm going to be late getting to the studio as it is."

After the dismissal bell, Fran fairly flew down to Mrs. Suder's room, only to find Millie there just outside the door. She refused to leave. "A lawyer defends an innocent person until he's proven guilty," Millie insisted. "Well, I'm your lawyer!"

Mrs. Suder was grading papers when the two girls entered. Her greeting smile quickly dissolved into a frown. "Millie McArdle— I wasn't aware that you and Fran are friends—"

"Fran's my very best friend," Millie began without preamble. "I'm here to plead her case, because I know that Fran won't defend herself."

The teacher's face was immobile as she gestured the girls to seats near her desk. She got up and walked over and stood beside them. "Millie, this doesn't concern you, no matter how close you and Fran may be. She was inexcusably rude in my class today, and she's here to be reprimanded."

"Mrs. Suder," Millie exclaimed, "Fran's so worn out she could fall asleep anywhere! She works after school and on weekends," Millie hurried on, "at Prince's Photo Studio, and they're having this Christmas rush. Her mother works full time at Draper's so Fran has to help take care of two sisters and a little brother. All that," she added defiantly, "should be enough to make anyone fall asleep in class!"

The teacher was searching Fran's face. "I see," she said quietly. "And your parents approve of this schedule? I suppose, since your mother works, too, she hasn't noticed the effect all this is having on you." She shook her head sadly. "This craving for luxuries will surely be the disintegration of the American home!"

"Luxuries!" Millie jumped to her feet. "Fran's mother works because she's a widow and has to support her family. Fran's only trying to help out." Millie's voice broke off on a sob as she whirled about and ran from the room.

Stunned, Fran slowly shook her head. "I—I don't know what got into her, Mrs. Suder—"

More surprising than Millie's behavior was the teacher's sudden smile. "Fran," she said, "Millie was defending a friend. But her feeling for you seems closer to a sibling relationship."

"I know," Fran agreed thoughtfully. "Millie's an only child. We've sort of grown up together."

Mrs. Suder resumed her place behind her desk. "Fran, I'm not quite as unperceptive as Millie believes. We often disagreed when she was in my class last year, but I'm not easily disturbed over personality clashes. In short, I don't run to the principal about everything." Her gaze was fixed on Fran's face. "Now, if all that Millie said is true, then it would be cruel for me to punish you for rudeness, wouldn't it? But I must urge you, my dear, to cut down on your activities or else you're likely to fall asleep in other classes. Then you'd really have complications!"

"Yes, ma'am," Fran replied. She smiled now, warmed by Mrs. Suder's softened expression. "I'm really sorry it happened, but it won't again. That's a promise."

The teacher beamed. "Well then, Fran, you may go."

Millie was crouched at the bottom of the stairs. Traces of tears could still be seen on her face. "Fran, am I going to be expelled?"

Fran couldn't resist laughing at Millie's forlorn-looking face. "No, Millie. Mrs. Suder melted completely after you told her my sob story. She's not the least bit angry. In fact, Millie, she even understands you and why you sounded off. Imagine!"

Millie brightened then. She got up and brushed off her skirt. Fran handed her friend the books she had left behind in her flight. "I guess we've never given Mrs. Suder a chance to show that she has a heart. But now—well, I'm on her side."

Fran related the entire episode to Joe that evening as they chugged through the traffic on Kensington Boulevard. After she had finished, Joe remarked, "You live a charmed life, Fran. I've heard of Suder. She's plenty strict."

Fran waited uneasily for Joe to add that she could have saved herself all that humiliation today by giving up her job weeks ago. Instead, he asked about Diane's and Linda's progress with their lessons. Fran responded eagerly. "Oh, Diane never walks anymore—she pirouettes. And Linda gets up early even on Sunday morning and practices her scales."

Now, as they parked in the lot at Martin's, Joe asked Fran about Jamie's bicycle. "You're getting him a twenty-four inch, aren't you?"

"I don't think so. We just want a sidewalk bike."

Joe shook his head. "Fran, you'll be throwing your money away if you get that boy a sidewalk bike now. Jamie's nearly nine, and he's growing fast!"

Reaching the entrance of the store, he opened the door.

Fran walked inside ahead of him, feeling puzzled. "But Joe, he wouldn't be able to ride a larger bike. Why, if he wakes up Christmas morning and finds a bike under the tree that he can't even *ride*, it'll break his heart!"

Joe replied solemnly. "Not as much as outgrowing it in just a few months will hurt him."

In all the confusion, Fran didn't notice that a salesman had joined them until he asked, "What can I show you today?"

"I'm not sure," Fran blurted. "I came in to buy a red sidewalk bike, but now I'm told that my little brother would soon outgrow it."

The saleman nodded. "That's certainly possible. To help you decide, let me show you what we do have."

Fran followed the man to the left side of the store where a long line of bicycles was on display. The smell of new rubber mingled with the metallic odor of the chrome-sparkling vehicles that stood in bright rows of red and blue and green. They're all so new, Fran thought excitedly, imagining Jamie's delight.

The salesman slid out several bicycles in various sizes and prices and styles, pointing out the features to Fran and Joe.

"They're all nice," Fran declared. "I really don't see why one of the small ones wouldn't be suitable." She turned to Joe who'd been standing aside with arms crossed, as if determined not to intrude in the transaction. "Joe, Jamie could ride one of the small ones all alone."

"Sure, for awhile. But by next summer or even earlier, he'll be too large for it, and then he'll need another bike."

Stonily, the salesman inquired, "How old is the young man?"

"Eight," Fran said. "He's about this tall," she added,

holding her hand at a place just above the hip pocket of her jacket.

Joe heaved a sigh. "He's taller than that, and you know it."

"Joe," Fran burst out, "are you trying to help me or confuse me?"

"Look, I refuse to stand by while you throw away good money. Use some logic, Fran. It'll be spring before the weather's nice enough for Jamie to ride much. Meanwhile he'll be growing. And then there's the matter of skill—it takes kids months sometimes to ride well enough to spend much time on a bike."

Fran avoided Joe's eyes. "I can't think ahead until next spring," she said miserably. "I keep seeing Jamie's face on Christmas morning!"

"He'll have a ball with a big bike, Fran. I know because it happened to me. He'll work twice as hard to learn to ride one."

Staring at Joe, Fran decided that he must be convinced of what he said, or he wouldn't be so persistent. "Well," she admitted quietly, "it does sound sensible."

She glanced back at the salesman who was fidgeting with his order book. "Miss, would you like some more time to decide? There are other customers—"

Fran took a deep breath, suddenly aware that the decision would have to be hers because her mother was probably at the grocery store this very moment. "I'll take a big one," she told the salesman. Turning to Joe, she urged, "Pick one out for me, will you, Joe?"

While the salesman wrote down the necessary details in his sales book, Joe went over and selected one of the medium-priced bicycles, red with twenty-four-inch wheels.

As they drove homeward, Joe told her, "If it'll make

things easier, Fran, tell your mother that I'll come over Christmas morning and ride Jamie around on his bike and show him how to take care of it."

"Why, Joe!" Fran exclaimed. "Jamie will be so pleased that he won't care that he can't ride it alone!"

Joe parked in his driveway on Dozier Drive long enough to take down the bicycle from the luggage rack on top of his car and hide it behind the patio fence.

Driving down to Sandy Lane, Joe asked, "Should we set a time for me to bring it over on Christmas Eve?"

"Joe, I haven't the slightest idea. I'll just call you after we get Jamie in bed. That is, if you plan to be home."

He chuckled. "Leave my family on Christmas Eve? They'd disown me."

Wearily, Fran trudged up the porch steps, grateful that the day was almost over. Diane and Linda rushed up to her as she entered the living room. Even Jamie, who was lying on the floor before the TV, sat up. "Hey, Fran, a teacher called about you!"

Fran's heart sank. "A teacher?" she whispered hoarsely.

Her mother appeared then, obviously distressed. "Fran, Mrs. Suder called just a few minutes ago. It's the first call I've had about you since you've been in high school!"

It's too much, she thought. Her knees buckled as she sank down on the sofa. "Mrs. Suder called you?"

"She seems awfully understanding, Fran," her mother went on, "but she was so concerned about you. She said that no amount of money is worth what you're going through! It upset me terribly. I didn't know you were so worn out that you couldn't stay awake in class!"

Fran wavered between giggles and tears. It was so ridiculous now. "Mother, all the kids want to sleep in that class. It's right after lunch, and Mrs. Suder just talks and talks. I just made the mistake of resting my head on my books, that's all."

"That's all?" her mother countered. "But she called personally to tell me!"

Fran got up and headed for the kitchen. "I'm starved, Mother. Let's eat, and then I'll tell you exactly what happened. You see, it really did turn out all right."

"Yeah, Mama," Linda agreed. "We can eat while Fran tells us everything. I bet it'll be *exciting*."

15

A Joyous Christmas Eve

Waverly Park shopping center, Fran thought, resembled a gigantic toyland. The annual Christmas tree had been mounted on the mall and emblazoned with bright ornaments, and a mammoth Santa was driving a sled of eight reindeer across the roof of Draper's department store. All the way down the street, there were lavish window displays. Several stores piped Christmas carols to the shoppers on loudspeaker systems. At the corners, shivering Salvation Army lassies stood, vigorously jingling their bells and tambourines.

Pausing in the doorway of the studio on Wednesday afternoon, Fran smiled to herself, remembering how enchanted the children had been last evening when their neighbor, Mrs. Holley, had driven them up here to view the fairyland scene.

Now, inside, Barbara greeted her with a glowing smile. "Thanks for coming in early, Fran. I hope it hasn't inconvenienced you."

"Oh, no." Fran slipped out of her coat. "Millie's keeping the children for me. She's supposed to be wrapping gifts. Can't you just imagine all the help she'll have?"

"It's been awfully quiet," Barbara remarked, "considering that it's Christmas Eve. But I still haven't had any lunch. Greg's been in that darkroom all morning, trying to finish up."

After Barbara had left for the day, Fran realized why the studio was so peaceful. There were no customers to pose for photos. Only those who had to drop by for their last-minute Christmas orders came in.

Fran's thoughts kept skipping ahead to the evening, when she would give Joe and Millie their gifts. Millie planned to stay on at the house until Joe brought down Jamie's bike. "I might as well," her friend explained. "My folks are having an open house for all of Dad's business friends. Dull!"

Chris, who had been as busy as Fran, catering to the season's business at his father's store, had called the evening before to say that he would try to visit her late Christmas Eve.

At four, Greg emerged from the darkroom. After saying hello, he added, "Here they are—the last of the Christmas orders—fresh from the dryer. Finis!"

The stack made a sturdy slap as he dropped them on the counter. "If we hurry, we can have these labeled and stuffed into envelopes. Just five sets, all family groups, and they're supposed to be picked up after five o'clock."

Fran quickly collected all the necessary white slips, paper clips, and fresh manila envelopes. As they worked together, she was conscious of Greg's weariness. Every now and then he stopped to rub a hand across his face.

After a moment, she said sympathetically, "I'll bet you're glad this is all over, Greg."

He stifled a yawn. "As the saying goes, it was a tough battle, but we won! Of course, I couldn't have managed without you, Fran—and Barbara. It just proves how a crisis can bring out the best in people. I never dreamed Barbara would give up shopping sprees and dates and parties to help with all this—"

Fran shook her head. "You're the hero, Greg, really. You kept us both going. You were so confident about everything working out for the best."

Greg smiled. "Fran, circumstances forced me into this role, but you and Barbara pitched in voluntarily." He looked at her then. "It's all been worth it, hasn't it, Fran? When you've seen what your salary can buy, it sort of makes up for all the work. Besides, it's great for the ego to know you can do something just a little better than the average person can."

"Greg," Fran spoke up, "don't you believe that some people face up to responsibility better than others? They—" She stopped, suddenly ashamed that she'd had Joe in mind. As wonderful as he had been lately, how could she think so unkindly of him?

Greg was stamping a row of photos as he spoke. "The way I see it, Fran, it's a question of maturity. Either we accept responsibilities or we escape them. Now, when I was a kid, I could have had a generous allowance, but I earned my own money. I had a paper route, and I cut grass and cleaned gutters for neighbors. Whenever I needed money, it was a challenge to me to prove to myself that I could fight my own battles. But you can't tell about people. There's Barbara—she's never earned a dime."

Part of Fran's mind was absorbing Greg's words, the other was checking Joe against them. Joe had never had a paper route, and he'd seldom mowed lawns for neighbors. Since he'd been in high school, athletics had monopolized his time. Of course, she reminded herself, he'd been a lifeguard all summer at Waverly Park. Yet, the times Fran had seen him there, sunning, or diving, or even chatting with friends while on duty—well, it had looked more like fun than work.

Joe, Fran reflected, had never known a real crisis. No responsibilities had disrupted his easy-going routine. Was that what bothered her? Am I afraid that Joe isn't as mature as he should be?

By six o'clock, there was only one envelope of pictures lying on the counter unclaimed. "Mrs. Bill Benson," Greg read aloud. "Can't imagine why she hasn't come by. Fran, give her a quick buzz, and tell her I'll bring these by."

Fran assured the apologetic customer, who had assumed that the studio would remain open late on Christmas Eve, that Greg would personally deliver the pictures to her home.

The two rushed around and closed the studio. Greg whistled, exuberant over the end of the long weeks of work. The drive home was as gay as the Christmas lights that blinked at them from the windows of houses they passed.

When Greg pulled into Fran's driveway, he became serious. "Fran, Mother's playing Santa tomorrow. She'll bring your presents from all of us. I'll be over at Barbara's most of the day. Oh, yes, I'll pick you up at about seven-thirty on Saturday night. That'll give us time to get things settled before the dance starts. I hope you haven't forgotten we're taking pictures there."

Fran felt riveted to the front seat. "The dance?" The words came out with a croaking sound. "Saturday night?"

"Fran, you didn't forget—?"

"No, I—" She was glad that it was dusk and that Greg couldn't see the tears filling her eyes. "I didn't think that you were expecting me to help, Greg. I've already promised Joe that I'd go with him!"

Greg clapped a hand against his forehead in a gesture of frustration. "Forgive me, Fran. I've been so wrapped up in the studio that I never once thought of your going as a student. In fact, I was under the impression that we *had* discussed it, but I must have thought it over so thoroughly that I thought I had mentioned it." With a weary sigh, he started the motor. "Those things are so hectic—taking down names and addresses, collecting money, not to mention taking the pictures. Mother used to go with Dad, and later I went along."

Oh, dear! Fran felt numb all over. She felt as if she were betraying him. "Greg," she burst out, not daring to think of the repercussions, "I'll help you. It's part of my job, so I'll manage to be there. Joe will understand—"

"Please, Fran," he protested, "don't make a Simon Legree out of me on Christmas Eve. There's no real problem, anyway. All I need is a young girl who can read, write, and count change."

Instantly, she remembered seeing several girls at school dances in the past who would probably prefer to help Greg than be labeled wallflowers. "You shouldn't have any trouble finding someone," she reassured him, "but if you should get stranded, Greg, let me know. Promise?"

"Fair enough, Fran. And Merry Christmas!"

Walking into the house, Fran felt as if she had disposed of a heavy burden. She decided then that she would tell no one, not even her mother, how close she had come to having her holiday ruined. Dismissing the incident completely, she joined Millie and the children and shared Millie's amusement over Jamie's antics.

"But the children were little angels," Millie insisted. "Just funny ones." While her friend related the eventful day, Fran prepared a simple supper of leftover beef roast, salad, and spice cookies and cold milk.

Millie glanced over the table with an expression of awe. "It's delish, Fran! How do you *do* it?"

"Practice, my dear. Necessity is the mother of invention and the father of practice, to paraphrase Mrs. Suder. In short, you learn to do what you have to do!"

The meal soon became a gala affair when Mrs. Avery arrived, laden with mysterious bundles—and ice cream.

At last, Fran and her guest cleared away the dishes. Reluctantly, Jamie trudged to bed, and Linda and Diane began to carry an assortment of strange, gaudy packages from their room to the Christmas tree in the living room. Afterward, Fran added her pile of gifts, and Diane and Linda made a game out of guessing their contents. At ten o'clock, Fran coaxed the giggling pair to bed.

Then she telephoned Joe. He was soon there, ripping away the paper to reveal the shiny red bicycle, flashy with chrome and sturdy on its balloon tires. Satisfied that it was ready, Joe stood it at a prominent angle in front of the glistening tree.

"It's beautiful!" Millie said quietly. "Jamie will be speechless!"

Flushed with excitement, Fran's mother served punch and fruit cake, and the four relaxed for awhile, sharing food and conversation.

Presently, Joe excused himself and went outside to his

car, returning with several tinseled packages. "I brought yours in too, Millie," he said impishly, "so don't look so envious."

"You have a gift for me?" she asked in mock surprise.

"All right, play the clown! You know we three haven't missed exchanging Christmas gifts since kindergarten. Of course, if you'd like to stop—"

"Oh, no you don't!" Millie snatched the package Joe had waved tauntingly in front of her. Tearing away the silver foil, she gasped, "My hero! Such a *huge* box! How did you know I liked Stuart's chocolates?"

"Because you've hinted constantly for weeks," Joe replied. He handed a package to Mrs. Avery. "This is for you." To Fran, he added gently, "Last, but not least."

Mrs. Avery lavished words over Joe's choice of dusting powder for her. "Lovely, just lovely!"

Fran began to show Joe the gifts the children had for him. "Millie opened hers tonight before the children went to bed, but they'll give you yours tomorrow."

Millie proceeded to describe the calendar Jamie had labored over at school and the bookmarks Linda had fashioned out of ribbon. She reopened the box with the white lace handkerchief that Diane had bought her because it was so "glamourous." Millie said with a twinkle, "I think Diane has a pocket knife for you, Joe. But be surprised, hear?"

Finally Joe concentrated on the gift Fran had given him. As he opened it, a grin spread across his face. "Just what I've always wanted!" he teased. "Say, how did you know I like march music?"

"Elementary," Millie broke in. "You're always whistling something by Sousa, and you turn up your car radio whenever a march tune comes on."

Millie was ecstatic over the woolly stole Fran had selected for her at Draper's. "Fran, it's luscious!" She slipped it across her shoulders, then cavorted about in front of them.

"Well," Fran spoke up then, "I fooled you both. You two were expecting me to give you photographs—one of Prince's Christmas specials—weren't you?" After the laughter subsided, Fran's mother urged her to open the gifts from her guests, adding, "Before I burst from curiosity."

Millie's gift was a pale pink blouse, one that Fran had admired in a store window one day when they had lunched together. "Oh, Millie, you shouldn't have! Just because I liked it—well, it was much too expensive."

Joe's gift was professionally wrapped. Fran recognized the paper. It came from Meade's, the exclusive jewelry store at the shopping center. With her heart thudding heavily, she whipped aside layers of crisp, white tissue paper until she was staring down at a gilded metal box with an elaborately etched design on the lid. Curiously, she lifted the lid and was startled when a melody came tinkling forth.

"A music box!" Millie gasped. "Fran," she squealed as she peered over the maze of paper, "it's gorgeous!"

With trembling fingers, Fran separated the object from the surrounding cardboard. "'Begin the Beguine'?" she asked, meeting Joe's eyes.

His voice was husky as he told her, "It's supposed to be a jewelry box. The music is just an added feature."

Fran set it down on its four knobby feet. "Oh," she said, fingering the soft, velvety interior. It was large enough, she noticed, to accommodate several necklaces and bracelets. "Thanks, Joe. I love it!"

Joe had to leave shortly afterward, and Millie accepted his offer to drive her home. Once she and her mother were alone, Fran held the music box in her lap and lifted the lid again.

"Fran—" Her mother's voice broke into her reverie. "I

hope you didn't mind my staying in here while you three opened your presents. The truth is, I keep forgetting you are no longer children. I sat there thinking back over the years and all those gifts—coloring books, jackstones, pens, puzzles, lockets. And those detective books Millie loved so!" In a gentler tone, she added, "I hope Millie wasn't offended at the difference in your gifts, Fran. I doubt if Joe realized how it looked, but I'm sure one of those music boxes is far more expensive than Stuart's chocolates."

"I know," Fran agreed, her throat tightening as she remembered Joe's tender expression. "Mother, could Millie be right? I mean, could a boy like a certain girl and not realize it?"

Fran's mother smiled. "There's no doubt that Joe's fond of you, dear. But you two have years to decide how you feel about one another. I think you're both being sensible dating others. And that reminds me—what happened to Chris?"

"Oh, it's much too late for him to come over now, Mother. He wasn't positive he could get away because his family was having a get-together."

"Well, then," Mrs. Avery declared as she unplugged the twinkling tree lights, "I'm going to bed. Christmas is a long day for mothers."

16

A Christmas Surprise

Fran had just entered the kitchen to help her mother get dinner started when the doorbell buzzed through the house. "It must be Chris," she said. "He's the only person who hasn't visited us today!"

All morning, she had been concerned about the welfare of the home-made, cardboard peppermint cane that was attached to the front door. Since dawn, it had swung with the constant swinging of the door.

Jamie had awakened and discovered his red bicycle at about six-thirty. By eight, Joe had arrived to give him a chilly but thrilling tour of Sandy Lane from the seat of his newest and most cherished possession.

Friendly neighbors and assorted children had dropped in to exchange gifts and to say a Merry Christmas. Millie had called twice, exuberant over her own portable TV and a new white coat with matching beret. Barbara had called to wish them all a Merry Christmas, and Fran had worked over the living room twice, collecting empty boxes, battered ribbons, and torn tissue paper.

Now, as she hurried to her room to freshen her make-up, she heard Diane answer the door. "Fran!" she called out, "it's Chris and he's got a present!"

Fran stiffened. Would Diane ever be subtle about anything? She smoothed her wool skirt and tucked in the pink blouse Millie had given her.

When she reached the living room, Chris sprang to his feet, handing her a red package bound with green satin ribbon. Grinning, he said, "Merry Christmas, Fran. Sorry I didn't make it last night, but Dad and I didn't leave the store until after ten, so we missed most of our own party."

He sat down on the sofa across from her, adding in a tone of resignation, "Every year Dad promises to close at six, but he always gets soft-hearted with these last-minute shoppers."

"Well, we missed you," Fran told him gently. "We had a nice party for four."

"What party?" Jamie burst out, turning from the TV set.

"Shhh!" Diane held her finger to her brother's mouth. "Stop interrupting, or Fran will send us out!"

"I will, anyway," Fran said now. "I didn't disturb you when your company came over, so let me talk to mine in privacy. OK?"

"OK!" Jamie grudgingly consented. "The play's all silly anyway. Hey, Chris," he added, "when you get tired of private talking, come out and see my new bike. It's on the back porch."

On her way out, Linda stopped in front of Chris and withdrew a slip of paper from the pocket of her sweater. "This is my very *best* present," she said, waving it gleefully as she handed it to him.

Chris read it aloud. " 'To Linda from Mother and Fran —one nice second-hand piano sometime next year. Three payments already saved.' " He chuckled. "Now that, Linda, is my idea of a great gift!"

After the children were gone, Chris picked up his present for Fran from the sofa where she had laid it. "Hurry and open it. I'm on pins waiting to see your reaction!"

Laughing at her forgetfulness, Fran began jerking at the bow. Then she gasped, "But I haven't given you yours!" She rushed over to the tree and brought back a red and silver striped box. "Everything's been so hectic this morning. A happy kind of hectic, though."

As she opened her gift, she decided that it must be something nice because Chris was wearing a smug smile. "Earmuffs?" Fran ventured, as she pulled out the strange furry object. "Why, they're beautiful!" Two fluffs of brown fur were attached to a curved rhinestone-bordered band. She rushed over to view herself in the mirror over the mantel. "Chris, this must be awfully nice fur. It's so soft."

"Only mink," Chris replied. "Can't you tell?"

"*Mink?*" Fran whirled around, aghast. "Chris, you—it's much too expensive."

"Don't worry, Fran, they weren't. Those earmuffs were a sales gimmick Dad got through an outfit that was trying to persuade him to handle a line of mink gadgets—you know, for sporting-goods customers to buy for the women in their lives without having to shop in another store. Anyway, Dad gave up the idea, so he gave me the earmuffs for my best girl, so—"

"Oh, Chris," Fran exclaimed, "it's the most wonderful gift I've ever had!" After the words were out, Fran remembered the musical jewelry box reigning so magnificently in the center of her dressing table. Well, it too, she thought, was the nicest and most wonderful gift, but in a different way.

Fran's mother wandered in. "Did I hear my daughter squealing with delight?"

"Look, Mother—" Fran tilted her head from side to side. "Mink!"

The word was like a signal, summoning the children back. Linda and Jamie came streaking in, and Diane beamed ecstatically over the fascinating gift. While the girls tried on the earmuffs, Chris finally opened his gift from Fran.

"Forgive the cliché, Fran," he said, as he fingered the rich black leather wallet, "but it's just what I needed. You're very observant, you know. My wallet was in shreds."

"I never noticed," Fran confessed. "I just thought you might like that one. It has special compartments for stamps and for special keys."

To the children's delight and Fran's astonishment, Chris slipped more packages out of his overcoat pockets. There was a set of binoculars for Jamie, costume jewelry for the girls, and cologne for Mrs. Avery.

The children took advantage of the party atmosphere to show Chris all their presents. Diane briefly donned her new white satin ballet shoes. "Mrs. King won't allow me to wear these but a few minutes a day," she explained to Chris. "I've got to serve my apprenticeship in soft slippers first."

Jamie tugged at Chris until he finally agreed to give an

opinion about the gleaming gift on the back porch. "Without a doubt," Chris conceded, "that's the handsomest bike I've ever seen, Jamie!"

Although the children begged Chris to join them for dinner, he had to decline. "We've got a turkey at home, and Mom's expecting me to eat most of it."

While they enjoyed the baked ham Mrs. Avery had chosen for the holiday meal, the children verbally concluded that Chris was as wonderful as Joe.

"We expected presents from Joe," Diane pointed out, "because we've known him forever! But Chris is new. Glory, I'd rather have mink earmuffs than a jewelry box, even a musical jewelry box."

While Fran and the girls were finishing the dishes, Mrs. Prince came by. Mrs. Avery welcomed her into the living room. Snatching off her apron, Fran hurried out of the kitchen and, as she entered the hall, overheard her mother inquiring about Mr. Prince.

"He's doing very well, Mrs. Avery," Mrs. Prince replied. "It's the first rest he's had in years, and it's been just grand for him."

Remembering how peeved her mother had been over the situation at the studio, Fran held her breath. Please, Mother, she thought, don't mention it now! But if Mrs. Avery blamed the Princes for anything, she failed to show it. When Mrs. Prince complimented her hostess on her charming family, Fran's mother said, "They're good children. I couldn't manage if they weren't. And Fran's a lifesaver for me."

"I can imagine," Mrs. Prince said now. "I don't know what we'd have done without Greg!"

Fran burst into the living room then, smiling as she greeted their guest. "Merry Christmas, Mrs. Prince! What a beautiful fur stole. Was this a Christmas gift?"

Mrs. Prince smoothed a hand over the soft fur. "Yes, dear, about eight years ago!"

There was more conversation, and then she turned to Fran. "Help me bring some things in from the car, please. I've felt like Mrs. Santa, delivering gifts all afternoon. I saved this stop for last, though."

The children soon gathered around them, tearing into the boxes of pajamas and toys. For Fran, there was a lovely sweater set, an imitation pearl necklace, and a purse—all gifts from the Princes. Barbara had included a small bottle of perfume.

Even Fran's mother received a soft coat sweater in a flattering shade of light blue. "You shouldn't have, Mrs. Prince," she kept insisting. "It's just too much!"

"Now, Mrs. Avery," the woman chided, "it was such a joy to buy children's gifts again. And I couldn't help remembering you. You've been so gracious about letting Fran help us out."

While the children played with their gifts, Fran fought back a pang of guilt. Overwhelmed by the Princes' generosity, she felt ungrateful. She just couldn't let Greg handle all those dance pictures alone.

When Mrs. Prince got up to leave, Fran handed her the three boxes of bedroom slippers she'd selected and wrapped so gaily for the Princes, along with a pair of sparkling earrings for Barbara.

"Mrs. Prince," Fran began unsteadily, "about the dance Saturday night— Tell Greg that I—I'll be glad to help him. I'll call Joe today and explain. I'm sure he can find someone else to go with him."

The woman gasped. "Nonsense, my dear! I was provoked at Greg when he told me he had mentioned the dance to you. But I suppose we can't expect a busy man to understand these things from a young girl's viewpoint."

She patted Fran's arm. "You go to that dance, my dear, and have yourself a wonderful time. Greg will manage fine."

"Yes, ma'am," Fran found herself promising, "I will."

When their guest had departed, Fran's mother turned to her with a bewildered expression. "What was that all about? Why were you even considering giving up the dance?"

Fran quickly explained the situation, pointing out that she had decided not to mention it to her mother once the crisis had passed. "It was just a mix-up, Mother. I'm going to that dance with Joe and have myself a glorious time!"

Mrs. Avery was gathering up the cardboard and paper litter scattered around the room. "Well, I'm certainly relieved to know that the crisis has passed. But I think you should have told me."

"And ruin your nice Christmas?"

"Ruin *my* Christmas? Oh, Fran, Joe has been so sweet and helpful to us that I'd have been ashamed to face him if you'd broken your date with him."

"I know, Mother," Fran agreed quietly. She picked up the mink earmuffs and studied them absently. "I'd have felt terrible. You know, Joe was right about Jamie and that large bike. Jamie was thrilled! And for Joe to come over to give him his first ride—well, it really was perfect."

17

The Holiday Dance

Saturday was as exciting to Fran as Christmas Day had been. Her emerald-green dress swung out from its hanger on the closet door, as glittering as any gem could be. Below it were the evening slippers that Millie had given her and Fran had redyed to match the dress. On the dresser, the long white gloves, a Christmas present from her mother, still nestled in their box, protected from prying fingers.

After lunch, Fran shampooed her hair and put it up ever so carefully on big rollers. She manicured her nails and dozed on the sofa until the polish was thoroughly dry.

At last the evening meal was over, and Fran began to

enjoy the results of all the weeks of planning. One by one, she slipped into the special garments and then began applying her make-up. The children formed an audience around her dressing table.

"Fran," Linda exclaimed in a tone of awe, "you look so beautiful!"

"Yeah, Sis," Jamie agreed. "Boy, won't Joe be surprised? He's never seen you dressed up!"

Fran made a playful grimace at her brother. "Never?"

"Jamie's right, Fran," Diane said worriedly. "You look so *different*. Maybe Joe won't like you this way."

Fran stared in dismay at her reflection. She'd been pleased with the effect.

"Shame on you, Diane!" Mrs. Avery said as she entered the room in the wake of Diane's reaction. "Your hair's lovely, Fran. It's just a little shorter and higher than usual."

"But is it too different?" Fran asked.

"Of course not! You look lovely, dear."

And soon afterward, Joe expressed his opinion in one exuberant "Wow!"

Fran quickly forgot herself as Joe absorbed her full attention. His unruly copper-colored hair had been conquered and smoothed into a becoming side wave. The black dinner jacket and trousers were far more sophisticated than any of the suits she had seen him wear. "Joe," she said, trying to control her smile, "you look wonderful."

His smile widened into a grin. "Thanks. For a minute there, I was afraid you were planning to swap me for someone else." He pushed a white box into her hand. "White camellias."

With deft fingers, Fran's mother ceremoniously pinned on the corsage. She took her best black coat from the entrance closet and slipped it around Fran's shoulders.

There was a flurry of good-bys, then the chugging roar of Joe's car, but above it all, Fran heard only the tom-tom pounding of her heart.

Except for the Linden-Carter wedding, the Holiday Dance was the most extravagant affair Fran had ever attended, as she soon discovered. She'd gone to several formal dances and numerous sock hops, but this one surpassed them all. As they walked across the school parking lot, Fran noticed that it was crowded with cars.

"Joe, I've never seen so many couples at a school dance before. I mean, at a formal one."

"We expected a big turnout, combining the two dances this way."

Fran looked at him in the light pouring out from the windows of the gymnasium. "What two dances?"

"You know, the Holiday Dance and the Junior-Senior Prom. Say, didn't you know about it?"

Fran shook her head, bewildered. "No. When was this decided?"

"It was explained in the postponement notice on the bulletin board. The faculty and the student council agreed that since the new auditorium would still be under construction in the spring and the gym in debatable condition from repairs, we kids might get cheated out of the Junior-Senior Prom."

Fran felt a sense of loss, as she had several times when she'd returned to school after vacation and discovered familiar things changed. She knew, of course, why she hadn't read the bulletin board announcement. She'd been so busy these weeks. Why, she'd scarcely had a conversation with anyone at school—even Millie, except about Christmas. She dismissed it now, though, with a casual, "I really have been hibernating, haven't I?"

Girls in formal dresses and boys in their rented tuxedos

were streaming toward the doors of the gymnasium as Fran and Joe entered. In the foyer, couples clustered in bright circles that suddenly widened when new friends arrived.

Fran glanced, fascinated, around the gym. Silver and gold baubles bounced from white satin ribbons looped across the ceiling. Now and then a steel pole had been wrapped in white ribbon and topped with a wrought-iron post light. She recognized several classmates, and then she spotted Millie pushing toward her, pulling Pete Cassidy along with her.

"Fran, how scrumptious you look!" Millie exclaimed.

"Thanks, Millie, but look at you!" Fran replied, admiring her friend's dark hair, sleekly fastened with a velvet ribbon that matched the powder-blue hue of her dress.

The congenial foursome soon became a huddle that was blocking the doorway until Joe broke away and led Fran across the gym, where they settled at a table among some of Joe's basketball pals and their dates.

Fran completely forgot Greg until a young couple passed by, discussing the photographer who was setting up his equipment out in the side foyer.

Joe turned to Fran. "Want to take a look?"

Fran nodded eagerly. Before they could make a gracious exit, however, the small combo arrived and the music began.

With her hand clasped tightly in his, Joe pulled Fran out into the maze of dancers. Eventually they wound their way around the fringe of the group until they were near the foyer on the left side of the gymnasium. Then they stopped dancing and walked.

Greg could be seen in the doorway, operating a camera attached to a tripod. Fran studied the young people assembled around him, but there was no one helping him. One couple stood at the end of the area, posing before a back-drop that consisted of a post light adjacent to a cardboard "building" prop. Near them, other couples were forming in line, waiting their turn.

"Well," Joe said absently, "we could have our picture taken now and have it over with."

Fran shook her head. "No, Joe, not yet. I mean, Greg's too busy right now."

"He'll be busy all night, so what's the difference?"

"That's why it bothers me," Fran confessed. "I was supposed to help Greg—if I hadn't come with you."

Joe was frowning. "But what could you do? The customers seem to be waiting on themselves."

"I know," Fran agreed, "but he could use someone to collect the money."

For a few minutes, Fran observed Greg's struggle to write names down on a large manila envelope, count out change, pocket the money, and direct each couple into a proper pose.

"It wouldn't be so much trouble," Joe spoke up, "if he didn't spend so much time on them. He can't be making much money on those pictures."

"But, Joe," Fran explained, "the amount Greg charges is just a token price. It barely pays for the supplies he uses. But his father's been doing these dance pictures at Waverly for years, and he—well, he doesn't like to charge teen-agers much. And Greg said it wouldn't be fair not to give them the best possible picture for the money."

Abruptly, Joe tugged at her arm. "It isn't your problem, Fran, so forget it. We're wasting all that great music!"

Fran smiled up at Joe, as he led her back to the dance floor. After all, she reasoned, I am Joe's date, so I owe him —not Greg—my attention. Then it came to her what a ridiculous turn of events it really was. For months, years really, she had dreamed of going with Joe, being his date at something important like this, so that everyone at Waverly could see them together. And now, though her heart told her she belonged in Joe's arms, her conscience wouldn't let her enjoy it.

Almost immediately Chris cut in. "You look terrific, Fran." He smiled down at her with a disconcerting twinkle in his blue eyes. "Having fun?"

"Of course! I saw you come in with Patty Mitchell. She's a doll, Chris. You couldn't have picked a nicer date."

He was grinning now. "Everyone's entitled to his own opinion, but I will concede that Patty's a doll."

Another boy broke in and, after him, still another. Finally Joe was there, teasing Fran about her popularity. "See what you've been missing all these months that you've played hermit?"

"Maybe that's the reason for it," she told him demurely. "Because I *haven't* been around lately."

Fran enjoyed the attention, yet her eyes kept wandering toward the foyer. She knew now, of course, that there would be no one to assist Greg. Because only junior and senior couples had been allowed to attend, there were no unescorted girls. I should help him, Fran thought miserably. She missed a step—the third one, in fact—and stubbed a green satin toe against Joe's thick shoe.

His arms fell away, and he stood there searching her face. "Look, why don't we just hike out there and ask the guy if he needs any help?" Without waiting for her answer, he grabbed her hand and ran interference through the whirling couples.

"Please, Joe," Fran protested, "don't spoil your evening. I'll forget all about it. I promise!"

Joe's chin was a firm line as he came to a halt in the foyer.

"All right, then," Fran conceded, "I'll stay out here and help, if you'll promise to join your friends."

"These *are* my friends," Joe retorted, with a sweeping gesture of his hand that included the couples gathered in the foyer.

As they viewed the confusion together, Fran began, "You see, Joe? Greg can't handle all this work alone!"

"Well, this line has to keep moving, Fran," Joe declared. "There are more than a hundred and thirty-five couples here tonight."

The camera clicked again, Greg called "Next," and another couple stepped up. All went well until the pair walked over to the backdrop. After several false starts, Greg had to arrange the boy's hands around the girl's waist, and her arms so that they curved gracefully around her bouffant skirt. "Now, hold it," Greg called out firmly, "and smile!"

The next couple presented a different problem. The boy clutched his partner much too tightly. "Look, cave man," Greg teased, "you don't want everyone to think you had to drag her to the dance!"

Suddenly, Joe turned to Fran. "What are we waiting for? The guy needs help!"

"*We*?" Fran asked incredulously.

Joe shrugged. "Why not? We've been dancing all evening."

Greg's face registered surprise and then delight when the two confronted him. When they offered to help, though, he objected. Joe quickly convinced him that they would enjoy the task.

Greg took a moment to explain that because the boys

usually paid for the pictures and picked them up after they were printed, only the boy's name and address was necessary.

While Fran managed this chore, Joe separated the males from their money. "All right, brother," he'd tell them with his impish grin, "hand it over!"

He maintained a lively flow of chatter that erupted now and then into hearty laughter. Soon, one of the teachers who was chaperoning the dance appeared. "My word," she exclaimed, "I never realized that taking pictures could be so amusing!"

"Say, Miss Phillips," Joe teased, as he turned his charm on her, "you're just the person we're looking for! How about posing right now for the picture you've promised us for the yearbook?"

Miss Phillips consented rather self-consciously. "Now, if this doesn't come out right," she warned Joe with a twinkle, "I intend to have it made over again!" Then, as she left, she cautioned the group to keep their voices down so that the talent skit being presented in the gymnasium could be heard.

Presently, Fran looked up into Betsy Parker's radiant face.

"Surprise!" Betsy cooed enchantingly from a cloud of red chiffon. She gripped the arm of a lanky young man whom she quickly introduced to Fran and Joe as Larry Tatum, a cousin who had come back from New York with Betsy and her family to spend the remaining holidays in Waverly.

"We've been watching your antics, Joe," Betsy said now. "You're certainly a good sport about everything."

After Greg had captured Betsy's smile on film, she led her escort away, pausing briefly beside Joe and Fran to urge, "C'mon with us, Joe. You don't want to remember your last big dance at Waverly like this! Fran can paddle her own canoe."

Joe playfully untwined the girl's hand from his arm. "I'm having a ball right here, Betsy. Thanks, anyway."

Fran had no time to be offended by Betsy's remark. On and on the couples came. Some of them stepped before the backdrop in proper, dignified poses, others ducked their heads shyly. Fran had to turn down several hems and way-ward ruffles and subdue boisterous boys and giggling girls. She even teased a few couples out of arguing over how they wanted to pose.

When the line dwindled down to two couples, Joe walked over to Fran, who was numbering some of the names she had written down rather hastily on a third ma-nila envelope.

"We've just finished with couple number one hundred and fourteen, Joe. Apparently, not every couple buys a photo."

"I guess not," Joe agreed. "I'm sure Greg doesn't mind."

When the last couple left, Joe steered Fran over to the backdrop. "Make it quick, Greg," he called over, "and painless." Standing on her left and gently holding her waist, Joe whispered against Fran's ear, "Now smile, tooth-less—*smile*!"

Of course, the shutter snapped just as Fran dissolved into giggles.

"Now that," Greg mused, "makes my evening worth-while!"

At a quarter to one, Joe parked in Fran's driveway. He got out and walked around to her door and helped her out. The lamp burning in the living room glowed across the grass as they neared the porch. Walking up the steps, Fran felt a strange sadness creeping over her. The Holiday

Dance was over and, with it, the Junior-Senior Prom. It was her first dance with Joe since the tenth grade and probably her last. Although he had insisted he'd enjoyed himself, Fran was still haunted by Betsy's remark.

"Joe—" Fran began. "It was wonderful of you to help me—help Greg, I mean. Really, I can never make it up to you, but I feel as if I must have ruined the whole evening for you—"

"Great day!" His tone implied that her suggestion was absurd. "I had a ball, and you know it."

"But Betsy—"

He had been holding her hand casually. Now he cupped it in both of his. "Betsy doesn't understand such things, because— Well, she wouldn't have pitched in to help anyone in a spot like that. I know one thing for sure—you were a good sport, Fran."

"Oh, Joe!" The words escaped in a rush of joy. There was more, so much more she wanted to say, but it suddenly choked in her throat. I can't cry, she thought; I can't go to pieces now!

Joe filled the gap by moving closer and kissing her, a tender quick peck at the corner of her mouth.

"Good night, Fran," he said huskily. "See you later."

Fran stepped inside the house and closed the door. She leaned against it while hot tears spilled over her burning cheeks. Joe had taken her to the dance, and he had gallantly rescued her from a crisis—and he had kissed her. But the humiliating part of it was, it had been a "brother's kiss."

Well, she knew the truth now. She and Joe could build tree houses together, buy bikes together, assist with a hundred and sixteen photographs at a high school dance, but to Joe she was still just a good sport!

18

Fran Considers her Future

As January went by, Fran decided that she might as well live a thousand miles from Joe because she saw him so seldom.

Shortly after New Year's, Joe's jalopy had collapsed from exhaustion and been hauled to a garage for repairs. Betsy Parker immediately included Joe in her exclusive car pool, leaving Fran and Millie without a ride until Chris graciously invited them to ride with him each morning. Moreover, he waited for Fran every afternoon after school and dropped her at the studio on his way to work. To confuse everyone thoroughly, though, Chris dated Patty Mitchell as often as he saw Fran.

Resigned now to her unimportant status in Joe's life,

Fran felt relieved to be spared that early morning ride in Joe's car. She missed the camaraderie that the three had enjoyed for so long, but the atmosphere in Chris's car was refreshing. Instead of sarcasm and sometimes dubious compliments, there was just his quiet good humor.

Even Millie behaved differently, Fran noticed. She was more polite and reserved. But then, Millie had recently replaced a drop-out on the cheerleading team and was engrossed in her new activities.

True to Greg's promise, business at the studio dropped amazingly after New Year's. Some afternoons dragged by with scarcely a phone call. Fran filled the time filing away negatives, bringing records up to date, and dodging the buckets and ladders belonging to the painters whom Greg had hired to freshen up the reception room.

In contrast to the studio, though, school created more work. More themes and book reports were assigned, and various committees sprang up to direct the vital decisions concerning the yearbook and the graduation program. Fran thought of herself now as a graduate-to-be instead of just a senior.

Barbara accompanied Greg on most of his weekend wedding commitments now. And on some Saturdays he actually closed the studio by two o'clock, so Fran was able to catch up on neglected chores at home.

One weekend she cleaned out her closet and completely rearranged it. Later, she did the same to her bureau, presenting the girls with a box of old costume jewelry that had seen better days. Another weekend, she supervised Diane and Linda while they restored their room to order. The improvement so pleased the girls that they eagerly joined Fran in launching a spring cleaning plan that promised to result in a spotless house by autumn.

Fran earned less money now, but she was pleased to have

the luxury of time off. Several Friday nights, she and Chris managed to attend basketball games. Then, after the games, they munched pizzas with Millie and Pete Cassidy. Pete was a star player on the varsity basketball team. They attended Youth League, too, usually joining a party later at someone's home. Those Sunday-evening gatherings afforded Fran the only lengthy glimpses she had of Joe. Fran knew, of course, that he was dating other girls besides Betsy Parker. But according to the date-by-date reports that Millie supplied, Betsy was still in first place.

Fran became aware of the difference in the conversation around her. There was a serious tone, a finality in the words of friends, particularly when they mentioned future plans.

On Valentine's Day, Millie invited her closest friends and their dates to a party at her home. Joe escorted Betsy, and Chris took Fran. Laura Maynard and Kit Kellogg were accompanied by two classmates.

Fran wore her red wool suit, one she'd bought out of her Christmas over-time money. But the others appeared in swishy silk frocks—except Betsy, who attracted much attention in a startling black velvet sheath.

Because all the guests were seniors, the banter soon became a lively discussion of the pros and cons of local colleges. Suddenly, Millie interrupted the conversation by turning to Fran. "Did you know that Betsy has been accepted at State U., too? Now there will be four of us—Joe, Betsy, Pete, and I."

"Really?" Fran managed. "How—how wonderful!"

Millie was smiling rather wistfully. "Oh, Fran, why don't you try to go with us? You're breaking us up, you know. You and Joe and I have gone all the way through school together!"

When the others glanced her way, Fran felt as if her

face had burst into flame. "Millie, I—I haven't saved enough money," she confessed. "In fact, I may keep working at the studio and just go to evening college."

"Evening college?" Millie was aghast. "Fran, don't you realize that only drips do that? There's no social life, no nothing! Besides, I thought you considered the art department at State U. one of the best."

"I do, Millie, and I might go there eventually. But it takes years to prepare for such a career, and right now—well, I'm not certain what I want to do." She lifted her chin a little as she added, "I have my family to consider, too, and my mother still needs me. If I go to evening college, I can stay here."

There was silence until Kit spoke up. "Well, I think girls should just take a business course and get office jobs. We'd certainly save our parents a lot of money. After all, most of us will be getting married, so why sweat out a college degree?"

"Let's not go through *that* again!" Laura pleaded. "We've had too many pep talks about the advantages of education. We all know," she added facetiously, "that it will make us better mothers and housewives."

"Not according to my mother," Kit countered. "She claims she uses more sixth-grade arithmetic than any course she had in college."

The group responded with chuckles, but Fran couldn't even smile. "Kit," she began in a low, unsteady voice, "if your mother was forced to earn a living, she'd be grateful for that degree. My mother got married the summer after she was graduated from high school. She didn't even bother with a business course, and now she's too busy to take any night courses, so the best she can do is saleswork. Of course, there's nothing really wrong with saleswork. It's just so *hard*."

"Now, Fran," Betsy chided playfully, "you're going at this the hard way. The smart thing is to marry a man who'll make a mint of money. Then you'll never have to lift a finger."

Pete slapped Joe on the back. "Well, that lets ol' Joe off the hook right there!"

The others burst into laughter while Joe sputtered until his face grew pink. Millie got to her feet. "Keep laughing, kids! All this talk about work and security makes me feel decrepit. Honestly, Fran, I admire you tremendously, but I can't pretend that I'm going to college for the sake of my future. I want to have some more good times while I'm still young!"

As Millie enlisted Laura's help to bring in the refreshments, Fran leaned back in her chair and tried to relax. It was then that she noticed Joe's dark gaze focused on her strangely, as if he'd never seen her before. I guess he hasn't, she thought—not on a soapbox at least.

Early Monday morning, Mrs. Rogers summoned Fran to her room. "My dear," the teacher began in a quivering voice, "*all* of our art-contest entries were returned. They didn't even make the semi-finals!" She reached over and gave Fran an affectionate pat on the arm. "I'm glad now that you didn't have your hopes too high. But I must admit, I'm heartsick over it."

Fran swallowed hard. She felt as shaken up as Mrs. Rogers sounded, but it must have been sympathy because, somehow, she felt a keen sense of release. "It really doesn't matter, Mrs. Rogers. I'll have other chances. After all, I didn't spend months poring over those paintings."

"You're right, my dear," the teacher agreed. "Of course, we received a lovely letter. There were thousands of entries, they said—thousands!" Soon she was reassuring Fran that the contest outcome was no reflection on her talent. "I'm sure it won't discourage you. Don't let it! Have you made any plans for after graduation?"

"I've thought about it a lot lately, Mrs. Rogers." Fran explained her present desire to attend evening college. "Or perhaps junior college. It will depend on what working hours I have. Along with secretarial subjects, I'd like to study advertising layout."

"Why, that's very sensible, Fran! You could start out in an agency and still continue with your art studies. My, I wish all my students could manage their lives as well as you have this year."

That evening, when the ten o'clock stillness settled over the living room, Fran laid aside her English textbook and told her mother about the sad return of the art entries.

Mrs. Avery had been patching a pair of Jamie's blue jeans. Now she looked up, startled. "Fran, how awful!"

"Now, Mother, you know I wasn't counting on that contest! But I feel as if I did win a prize." She repeated the teacher's words. "I guess that meant more to me than anything. Lately, with everyone talking about college, I—well, I feel as if I'm a freak or a failure."

"Fran, you're a marvel. There were times," her mother continued, "when I could have cried for you, and other times when I was exasperated. But you were always an inspiration."

After a pause, her mother looked up. "Fran, you won't feel left out this fall when Millie and Joe—all your friends—leave without you? I think this has been the hardest part of all for me. I feel so guilty for being unable to send you to college."

"Mother," Fran broke in, "I'll do just fine. Who knows?

I may wind up being a photographer, or I might really become the artist Mrs. Rogers thinks I could be. Why, when I count all the wonderful people who've helped and encouraged me this year, how can I feel discouraged about the future?"

19

A Friendship Sealed

"Now, Fran," Millie teased that Saturday morning, "you should let me in ahead of everyone else. After all, I'm your very best friend!" She put her arms on the counter and smiled dramatically into Fran's face.

"Of course, Millie," Fran mocked. "Just take a seat and I'll sneak you in somewhere." Two girls snickered, and across the room, another young girl opened a white box that emitted sweet smells of freshly baked brownies.

Fran studied the customers in the reception room. All of them were students who'd waited until a week before the deadline to have their photos made for the Waverly High yearbook. Millie had suddenly decided that now, in March, her hair style was prettier than the one she'd worn last December, so new photos were imperative.

"Mind my standing here bothering you?" Millie added impishly. "Of course, it wouldn't make any difference—"

Fran laughed indulgently. Squaring her shoulders, she replied, "I have the situation under control."

"So I see." Millie shook her head, so chic now with dark, feathery curls. "Honestly, Fran, I wish I had some of your poise. Why, you run this place singlehanded!"

"It's just confidence, Millie, based on experience—you know, practice." As she spoke, Fran was making future appointments on the desk calendar from the handful of notes she'd made during telephone calls.

When she came to the names of Joe Collier and Betsy Parker, Fran paused and took a slow, deep breath. This was the afternoon for their photos, too. Poise, she thought. At that moment, she felt about as confident as a wet negative. She'd hardly seen Joe for weeks, but she'd heard all the rumors. First, that he'd given Betsy his honor-society pin, which practically meant they were engaged. On the other hand, though, she'd been told that the two had quarreled and broken up. Still, they were seen everywhere together, particularly since they'd won two of the titles in the annual superlative contest.

Fran had tried to convince herself that Joe and Betsy could never be serious about one another, for they had so little in common. Then again, she had no idea what type of girl appealed to Joe. She only knew that she wasn't it. The telephone buzzed at her elbow, and she picked it up.

"Prince's Photos. Miss Avery speaking," she said, in a calm, direct voice. As she conversed with the caller, Fran told herself that she should feel confidence in her ability. Since last September, she had been confronted at the counter, and over the telephone, with every conceivable situation regarding photographs, and she had learned how to solve them.

Fran hung up, and Millie looked at her expectantly. "Anything exciting?"

"Just a woman asking for our prices."

The glass door opened then, and Millie turned. "Well, well," she whispered to Fran, "here comes Most Beautiful clinging to Most Popular!"

Fran forced a smile in the direction of Joe and Betsy, but to Millie she said, "They're here for photos for the year-book."

"I should have guessed," Millie retorted. She moved away from the counter and took a seat, but she peered over her notebook at the proceedings.

"Hi, Fran!" Betsy greeted her with a toss of her head. "Haven't seen you in ages."

Joe's voice was gentler. "We've been busy working on the yearbook," he said, as if to explain Betsy's remark. "How's Jamie doing with his bike?"

"Just fine, Joe," Fran replied. "He can reach the pedals now. You were right," she went on, above the clamor in-side her heart. "Thanks again for the expert advice."

Betsy was staring at them as if annoyed. Far more dis-concerting to Fran was Joe's grin and his brown eyes look-ing into hers. Quickly, she concentrated on the appoint-ment book. "We're running late this afternoon, so it'll be at least half an hour before your turn comes up. You'd have time to get a coke, if you'd like."

Betsy responded by linking an arm through Joe's. "C'mon, pet, you know you're famished."

Fran was relieved when the pair left, and she was glad that they didn't return until a moment before Greg was ready for them. She had to admit that she was uncomfortable when they were around, but she was certain that it wasn't jealousy. As Mrs. Suder would reason, because she no longer felt inferior to Betsy, how could she be jealous of her?

It's just me, Fran told herself now. After all this time, and with no encouragement, I'm still self-conscious around Joe. Well, she consoled herself, she wouldn't have to guard every word and glance much longer. In September, Joe would be two hundred miles away at college.

Chris was waiting for her at the curb at six-thirty-five. As they cruised down Dozier Drive, he interrupted their casual conversation. "Fran, I'll probably be late picking you up tonight. Dad wants me to help him with some stock at the store. And my mother's been shopping all day, so I'll have to grab a sandwich somewhere."

"Chris, have supper with us!" Fran exclaimed. "It's just meat loaf and potatoes—that is, if Diane put them in the oven on time."

He shook his head in protest. "I wouldn't dream of imposing on you like that."

"And I wouldn't dream of letting you eat a mere sandwich just so we can get to a movie on time."

The sound of Linda practicing in another room was barely audible above the clash of fencing swords in the TV movie that Jamie was watching. Then Diane appeared in a flash of blue satin. Balancing on her toes, she was struggling to tie an apron over a stiff skirt of tulle.

"Diane!" Fran gasped. "What are you doing in that costume?"

Diane's blue eyes were filling with tears as she stared at Fran and then at Chris. "I was just practicing, Fran! I've got to rehearse in a costume, sometime—!"

"But that costume doesn't belong to us! We only borrowed it so we could copy it!"

"Glory, Fran, I was only *practicing*!" She turned a

glowing smile toward their guest as he sat down on one of the kitchen chairs. "Hey, why don't you come to my recital, Chris? All the neighbors will be there and all the kids at school!"

"All right, Diane," Fran told her sister, "change your clothes now. I'll need you to set the table." She grabbed a pot holder and peeked into the oven. "If it tastes as good as it smells," she said, "it should be delicious. Meat loaf and scalloped potatoes are two of our favorite dishes, Chris. Mother fixes it in the evening and Diane shoves it into the oven the next afternoon."

Chris walked over to the back door and gazed out into the yard where sprigs of green were pushing through a layer of brown earth. "Your family has a nice place here, Fran. Our front lawn isn't much larger than our living room rug."

"Really?" Fran replied absently. Conversing with Chris while putting on a meal wasn't, she discovered, so simple as talking to her mother or the children while she did so. There were times while she was combining vegetables for the salad when she lost the thread of conversation.

Suddenly, though, one word attracted her attention. "Chris, I'm sorry, but I—I didn't hear that last remark."

Chris walked over to her. "I just said that I owe you a lot, Fran, for all your advice."

"My advice?" She was listening intently now. "About what?"

He strode back toward the table and straddled one of the chairs. "Don't you remember Millie's Valentine party? On the way home, I told you that my big dream was to be a lawyer, and you told me to just go ahead and do it. Well, I fought it out with myself for weeks. Then, the other evening, I faced Dad with it. Oh, he was furious. He thinks I should be grateful for the store and devote my

life to it. But I've never shared his enthusiasm for mer-
chandising. You see, Fran, if anything ever happened to
Dad and the store was left to me, I'd sell it in a minute and
go my way. So I'd be foolish to give up my personal plans
just to please him. Well, I finally convinced him and
smoothed things over. I'll be helping Dad in the store and
going to law school at night. It'll take me years, but it'll be
worth it."

Fran felt as if she were glowing all over. "Chris, I'm so
glad for you! It's just wonderful, really it is."

Mrs. Avery, her arms crammed with packages, stopped
in surprise when she found Fran, the younger children, and
their guest all assembled at the dining-room table, eating
meat loaf by candlelight. "Well, never a dull moment!" Her
smile brightened as she greeted Chris.

He stood up instantly. With a sheepish smile, he said,
"I'm afraid Fran has gone to a lot of trouble for me—"

"Paper napkins?" Mrs. Avery replied with a chuckle.
"I'm afraid she didn't go to enough trouble." She continued down the hall, but she soon rejoined them, looking
rested and comfortable in a cotton house dress and wearing
fresh lipstick.

"Mother," Diane spoke up immediately, "Chris has
promised to give me and Linda some constructive criticism.
You know, you and Fran aren't very helpful. You think
everything we do is perfect, but Mrs. King says—"

"Hey," Jamie interrupted, "I tell you the truth, and
that's that you're awful!"

"Glory, that's even worse!" Diane countered. "Everything we do is awful to you!"

Fran's mother glanced at Chris. "It's obvious that there's
been no lack of conversation, what with Linda's and Diane's
recitals coming up and graduation time here."

"This is quite a busy family, Mrs. Avery," Chris said. "Mine seems rather boring in comparison!"

After Chris had returned to the store, Fran rushed Linda and Diane through the dishwashing. Then she dressed, humming contentedly to herself. Chris is nice, she thought, and I really do like him. We have a lot in common, she reasoned, because we both have responsibilities. That's something Joe just wouldn't understand.

From her room, Fran could hear Linda and Diane pouncing on Chris when he came back, giving previews of their recitals. When she finally reached them, she made a gesture of helplessness. "Please excuse them, Chris. They perform for anyone who shows the slightest interest!"

"But I'm flattered," Chris insisted, his blue eyes twinkling. "I wouldn't miss those recitals for anything!"

He sounded so sincere that Fran sighed, resigning herself to the inevitable. It was obvious that Chris was filling the place that Joe had once had in the children's affections.

They drove into town to the opening of a new movie. It had been hailed as an exciting suspense story, but Fran found her thoughts wandering to her own problems. Is Chris really using the children to win me over? she wondered. But then she reminded herself that Joe had always adored the children—for themselves, no matter how he had felt about her. So, she decided, maybe Chris really is fond of them.

There I go, she thought, comparing Chris with Joe again. She supposed that it was only natural to compare every new boy with Joe. She'd never lived further than three blocks from him in all her life. The whole thing's elementary—Joe's probably just a habit with me, too.

20

Discovery

The month of May was a madhouse at the studio.

Scores of mothers brought in little girls who were students at Loretta King's School of Dance, hoping to capture them in graceful poses before they outgrew their fluffy, flashy recital costumes. Teen-agers from Waverly High poured in to sit for formal graduation photos suitable for relatives and friends.

There were brides, too. A few engaged girls preferred to have their pictures taken in their bridal finery before the flurry of late-hour parties began. Newlywed couples who had had small, informal weddings came in after their wedding day to have photos taken.

It was a red-letter day for Diane and Linda, the Saturday that they came to the studio, bringing Jamie with them, to have their own portraits taken.

The atmosphere in the reception room seemed gayer to Fran now, even more so than it had been at Christmas. After an extended rest, Mr. Prince had taken his place once again behind the portrait camera, releasing Greg to concentrate on darkroom work and outside photo assignments. Barbara helped Greg on many of the weekend weddings, but he and his father handled most of the larger ones together.

Fran dreaded the wedding that was scheduled for the last Saturday night before graduation. Barbara had already made other plans, so Fran had agreed to accompany Greg. On that evening, a cousin of Joe's, Dick Larson, was to marry Lucille Mann, his childhood sweetheart. Joe, who was three years younger than his cousin, would be an usher, and Betsy Parker, who knew Lucille quite well, was one of the bridesmaids.

As the days crept by, Fran overcame most of her apprehension. It no longer mattered to her how many classmates would be there to stare at her curiously. She was proud of her job; and, to her, a wedding seemed the most exciting part of her work.

As for Joe— Well, Fran told herself, she would be casual around him, just as she had for weeks now. There was really nothing to worry about.

Greg came by for Fran at seven o'clock. On the way, he explained that as far as he knew, the wedding would be on time. "I'm glad they picked a local church," he added. "At least I know where things are, and I'm familiar with the lighting problems. Fran, Lucy and Dick want me to take some color pictures, too. I'll use the 4x5 camera for black and white, but I'll want you to stay close with the other camera, so I can switch quickly. You won't forget, will you?"

"Oh, no," she promised. "I won't forget!" She was wondering how she would ever manage the strobe light and Greg's satchel, which was bulging with film, and another camera all at once. I'll be a walking camera supply store, she mused. But she really didn't mind.

The church was already filling with guests when Fran and Greg walked up the steps. Several classmates recognized her and waved gaily. When the two paused in the vestibule of the church, Fran glimpsed several members of Betsy's crowd, moving around near the flower- and fern-banked altar.

Greg stepped over to a room on the left and knocked on the door. "This is the church office," he explained. "The bridal party is supposed to be in here."

A pretty brunette in a dress of pale pink chiffon opened the door a crack. "Oh, it's you—the photographer!"

There was a murmuring of voices, and soon the girl stepped aside so they could enter the small room. A large desk had been pushed aside, and the remaining wall space was lined with folding chairs that were cluttered with clothes and boxes.

A woman was talking on the telephone, another was combing the blond hair of the bride-to-be, while a third was on her knees dabbing cleaning solvent on the hem of the bridal gown.

The bride stood before a mirror that was attached to a closet door, fidgeting with her veil. Sighting Greg, she whirled. "Oh, Mr. Prince!" she cried, "everything's gone wrong! I forgot my little white Bible—completely *forgot* it—so Mother went home for it. I'm afraid she won't make it back in time!"

"Now, Lucy," Greg chided gently, "we've got thirty minutes before the count-down." He turned toward Fran. "Lucy, this is my assistant, Fran Avery."

"Oh, I'm so glad to meet you, Fran! Betsy has spoken of you. She thinks you're so smart! And I'll be needing your help, too," she rushed on. "This is Dick's church, but we're not using his pastor or mine. Mother wanted us to have old Reverend Witherspoon, who married Mother and Dad and baptized me. Dad's supposed to meet him at the train. If they don't get back in time— How long is it proper to keep the wedding guests waiting?"

"As long as you have to!" Fran assured her. "It's your wedding. Don't worry about your Bible, Lucy. I'm sure we can find one downstairs in the Sunday School department."

"Could you? Oh, Fran, that would be wonderful!"

The pretty brunette in the pink dress stepped up to them. "Lucy, your parents could walk in at any moment. Shouldn't you go ahead with the pictures?"

"Oh, of course!" Lucy exclaimed, flustered. Quickly, she introduced the three aunts who were assisting her. The young brunette was Marsha Mann, one of Lucille's cousins. Then she explained to Greg some of the poses she wanted.

Greg began snapping photos of Lucille smiling into the mirror while Marsha adjusted the crown of pearls on her head. He took others of the aunts arranging the bouffant skirt, but the room was much too cramped to afford a variety of angles. Even more disconcerting to Fran and Greg were the interruptions.

Suddenly, Betsy Parker burst in, daintily pretty in her pink frock. With her were two more bridesmaids. "What's going on?" she asked, scanning all the faces in the church office. "The wedding's supposed to start in fifteen minutes!"

Marsha hastily explained why Mrs. Mann, who had insisted on supervising the final details, wasn't there.

"Oh, Marsha," Lucille burst out, "we can't wait that long to see to last-minute details! Betsy, would you please round up the wedding party and find Joe. He's with Dick."

Betsy shrugged. "That could be anywhere! C'mon, girls."

"Betsy," Fran called out as the trio reached the doorway, "would one of you go down to the Sunday School department and look for a small, white Bible? We'll use it in case Lucille's mother doesn't find hers."

Betsy stared in surprise, then she smiled. "Will do."

After that, Greg changed cameras and took a few pictures in color, with Fran holding the strobe light at all the necessary angles.

Presently, Betsy and her entourage surrounded them. With a flourish she held up a small, white, leather-bound New Testament. "We found it lying on one of the chairs," she explained. "Probably left from last week. We'll return it later."

"Oh, Betsy, *thanks!*" Lucille said fervently. "And thank you, Fran, for the touch of genius!"

Beyond the cluster of pink dresses, a tall form moved into the room. It was Joe, clad in dark trousers and a white dinner jacket, which reminded Fran, somehow, of the big Holiday Dance.

She stepped forward. "Joe," she said lightly, "to the rescue again! Would you mind organizing things so that when the Manns arrive, the wedding can start immediately?"

Joe's glance darted to Lucille. "Where did your mother go?"

The young girl's voice was shaking now. "There's no time to explain. How—how's Dick?"

"Last time I saw him, he was a wreck. I don't think he can hold up much longer." Joe disappeared then, with Betsy's group following.

Fran turned to the bride-to-be who was now close to tears. "Hold on a little longer, Lucy," she said gently. "Greg has weathered a lot of weddings, and they all work out right at the last minute, in the most wonderful ways!"

Ten minutes later, all the confusion ended in a joyous reunion in the vestibule. Mrs. Mann, rushing from a taxi, dashed up the church steps just behind Lucille's father, who had finally arrived with Reverend Witherspoon.

Greg preserved on film the precious moment when Lucille flung her arms about the kindly old man who had journeyed so far to perform the ceremony. When the two parents embraced their daughter, Greg's camera clicked away. A few moments later, Betsy signaled to the organist and the wedding began.

As Greg and Fran had expected, it was a smoothly timed and beautiful ceremony. There were no mishaps with the photographs, no awkward pauses. To Fran, it was really a momentous event, for she felt a poise that even surpassed the confidence she knew she had gained in the past few months.

Joe's mother, whom Fran hadn't seen for many weeks, had foregone the wedding to remain at the nearby country club and supervise the refreshments for the reception. It was there that Fran saw her, pouring punch into fragile crystal cups.

"Why, Fran!" Mrs. Collier exclaimed happily. "How nice to see you again!" Her glance embraced the camera that Fran was carrying. "You know," she went on, "Mrs. Prince is in my circle at church. She—all the Princes— think so much of you."

"Really?" Fran replied. She couldn't think of anything else to say, and when she noticed that Greg was beckoning to her, she excused herself and hurried away.

"They're going to cut the wedding cake now," Greg told her.

Fran responded by handing him the camera she held and accepting the 4x5 camera he gave her. While Greg worked, Fran became aware of Joe. He was standing near the swinging door that led to the kitchen area. He was alone, and he was watching her.

Flustered, Fran turned away. Later, when her eyes clashed with his, she smiled—a casual smile. To her astonishment, Joe returned her smile with a friendly wink, the kind she had often seen him give Betsy.

After that, she was conscious of his dark eyes following her throughout the gathering. Tugging at her mind was the memory of another evening when Joe's face had worn the same expression. Millie's party, she told herself now, when I preached from my soapbox! I wonder what I'm doing tonight that annoys him?

Greg now decided to concentrate exclusively on candid shots with the color camera, so Fran withdrew from the crowd. In a far corner, she found a bench tucked away behind a potted palm. Putting Greg's satchel on the floor, she sat down on the bench, carefully laying the 4x5 camera beside her. She considered slipping out of her high-heeled pumps, just to stretch her toes a moment, but then she heard footsteps approaching.

Soon, the sounds became the full-length form of Joe Collier, peering around the palm. "No wonder I couldn't find you," he teased. "You were hiding!"

Fran swallowed hard. Joe was the last person she would expect to find her there. "Is anything wrong? Is Greg looking for me?"

"No. I just wanted to talk. You've been so busy—"

"I know," she interrupted uneasily. Where is Betsy? she wanted to ask. Why wasn't Joe hovering over her or, at least, chatting with his relatives? "It—it was a lovely reception," she inserted, making small talk. "Your mother did a wonderful job."

He shrugged. "Who wouldn't have, putting in all that time?" He stepped over and picked up the camera and sat down on the bench. "Mind?"

"Of course not," she said.

He set the camera on the floor with a dramatic flourish. "Say, want some punch? You must be thirsty after all your rushing around—"

"No, thanks, Joe. I've passed the table so often that I've probably had more sips than the wedding guests."

Joe's eyes were probing her face. "Is Greg driving you home? Is that why you're waiting around?"

"Partly. I can't leave until he's through. Why?"

"Well, I just thought—"

Fran couldn't remember having seen Joe so ill at ease in years, not since those days long ago when she had teased him unmercifully. "Joe, are you trying to tell me something? I mean, is it about Betsy?"

His face clouded. "Great day! Why do you keep pairing us off? I've never dated Betsy any more than you've dated that Chris Watts!"

"I'm sorry." Fran managed unsteadily. "But I couldn't help it," she went on with a gaiety she didn't really feel. "After all, you've hardly spoken to me for weeks."

His eyes were level with hers. "Fran—just this once, could you forget everything before tonight? Look, it isn't late. I have to help Mom get some of these flowers home, but after that, would you like to go somewhere? There's a late show at the drive-in."

Fran shook her head. "It's much too late, Joe, and I've been working since this morning." She smiled. "Some other time?"

His voice was husky now. "You're different, Fran. I hardly know you sometimes. The rest of us—well, we'll probably be high school seniors at heart all the way through college. But you've grown up. You're so *sure* of yourself!"

Fran's smile widened. His words were an echo of other compliments that she had heard lately. Hearing Joe say it, though, touched her deeply. "Thanks, Joe, but I— Well, I suppose I had to grow up sooner than you and Millie. You know, I haven't said this to anyone before, but I've just realized that I took that job to help my mother and the kids—to give us all a few things we didn't have—but I really think I've got more out of it than anyone!"

Joe reached out for her hand and held it fast. "Fran, I know you won't believe this, but tonight, seeing you here — Well, it came over me—I'm going to be sorry about going away to State U. after all." His voice faltered. "Fran, promise me you'll write to me and save some dates for me when I come home for the holidays."

Tears were stinging her eyes, but she blinked them back. "I will, Joe," she whispered.

A moment later, Betsy Parker and the other attendants swarmed around them, eventually convincing Joe that his mother needed him to load up the station wagon with flowers. As he got up to leave, he said to Fran, "I'll call you tomorrow."

Betsy lingered for a moment, regarding Fran impishly. "I'm glad you two finally got together, Fran. Joe's been wild about you for ages. A girl can tell these things, even if a boy can't!"

She can, *how?* Fran thought, her eyes blurring from the joy of it.

Fran was certain of one thing as she left the country club with Greg a short while later. It was the most beautiful spring night she had ever seen. The stars were glorious, the air was glorious! I'll call Millie tonight, she told herself, and tell her that she's been right all along. "Millie," I'll say, "I'm no longer a habit from Joe's childhood. He doesn't think I'm a martyr, either. It's as if I'm someone new, someone he's just met!"

She realized then that Greg was speaking to her. "I'm sorry, Greg. I didn't hear you."

He chuckled gently. "It wasn't as important as your star-gazing, I'm sure. I simply made the observation that we took a mountain of pictures, but then that's entirely beside the point, isn't it?" He darted a grin at her. "And what will Chris say when he learns that he has a rival?"

"Oh, Greg, you don't miss anything!" she exclaimed. "As for Chris, he and I are just good friends. Besides, can't a girl as young as I am have two beaus at once?"

She couldn't tell Greg, of course, that one beau had long been her favorite. Anyway, she wanted to wait, to give herself time to discover whether Joe would be like someone new to her, someone she had just met.